Not a day goes by that I do not wonder why the Lord gave me such a willful child. He is far too much like his mama. I cannot help but imagine when I see him wander off toward places he ought not go if this is what You feel when I am tempted to do the same. Thank You, Father, for this precious son of mine and for loving me so much more than I can ever hope to understand.

—*from Prudence's diary*
May 1, 1860

Picture This

SECRETS OF WAYFARERS INN

Picture This

KATHLEEN Y'BARBO

Guideposts

New York

Picture This

Chapter One

May 1, 1860

Prudence and Jason Willard strolled down the path that ran alongside the Muskingum River toward Marietta with little Moses toddling along between them. At nearly one year of age, the child was already sturdy and well-built as a boy nearly twice his age, and he had been walking for more than a month.

Moses also favored his papa in determination. Today that trait showed itself in his demand to be allowed to walk rather than be carried. Each time Prudence hauled him into her arms, he wiggled out.

"Walk," he had learned to say almost as easily as he had learned the word *no*. At first she had encouraged the little one's independence. Today, she wished perhaps she had not.

Not a day went by that Prudence did not wonder why the Lord gave her such a willful child. Of course, the thought was always quickly followed by another: because he's a good match for his mama.

Thus they were making slow progress down a path that offered more dangers than tripping over a root or stepping into soft ground. For as much as Prudence worried about those things in light of her husband's injured leg, she also worried about what went on in the slave state of Virginia just across the river.

There had been talk of war for far too long for it to pass as rumor. Prudence cast a glance across the river and marveled once again at the land so like the place where she stood and yet so unlike it. Here she was free. There she would not be.

At the sound of rumbling, Prudence stopped to reach for Moses. Of course he made a fuss, but this time she ignored him.

"The child is too big for thee to carry him on such an uneven path," Jason protested as Prudence lifted their son onto her hip. "Best I do it."

Indeed, her husband spoke the truth, but she knew quite well that Jason's injuries would pain him even more were he to be the one to carry Moses. "Truly he is not a burden," she responded as she inclined her head to place a kiss on the boy's chubby cheek. "Does thee hear that?"

Jason paused to lift his ear toward the sky. "I do. It appears to be coming from the north, or perhaps just east of due north." He shook his head. "A curious sound, it is."

The rumbling got louder, and a strange whistling sound now accompanied the noise. "What is it, Husband?" she whispered.

He nodded toward the sky, seemingly unable to speak. "There," he finally managed.

Prudence followed the direction of his wide-eyed stare to look up at the deep blue spring sky. A fast-moving object streaked across the northern horizon leaving a trail of fire and wisps of white in its wake.

The ground shook beneath their feet, and Moses began to whimper. She reached for Jason with her free hand. "Has war finally come?"

The café area of the inn was a favorite spot for many in the town of Marietta, Ohio, but especially for LuAnn Sherrill, Tess Wallace, and Janice Eastman. The three were retired teachers, best friends, and the owners of the beautifully restored historic Wayfarers Inn. With its homey ambiance, its wide variety of yummy soups as well as teas and coffees, it was a natural gathering place for those who appreciated a delicious lunch, a relaxing atmosphere, and views of the river.

Today two of the three innkeepers were enjoying coffee after lunch and discussing an idea that had been in the making for a while: their very first Marietta First Friday event. While First Friday had become a tradition in Marietta, this was the first time the inn had been included in the monthly celebration of food, family fun, and the arts. All along the downtown streets, shop owners would be throwing open their doors after hours to offer their wares as well as to showcase art or food that would be added for the occasion.

LuAnn turned the page in her notebook to review her checklist. As the one who provided organization and her own dash of perfection in everything she did at the inn, she had been tasked with preparing for tonight's festivities. There were lists, spreadsheets, and a lengthy file on her computer dedicated to the event.

Still, she felt there were details that had escaped her. But then LuAnn often felt that way—thus the notebook and the checklists that kept her on track.

"It's our debut. Everything must be perfect," she told Tess.

Tess nudged her and grinned. "With you in charge, it's guaranteed. Besides, it's early. You have a couple of hours to go yet."

"Nothing is guaranteed," LuAnn said as she suppressed a shudder. "Especially since Grant keeps changing his mind about which photographs he wants to let us hang for the event. Doesn't he realize that one change affects everything else?"

At Brad Grimes's insistence, LuAnn had examined his younger brother Grant's collection of photographs and deemed them absolutely amazing. Since the event combined food and art, showcasing Grant's photos was the perfect choice. Now the photos hung all around the first floor of the inn awaiting purchase by First Friday shoppers.

Tess waved her hand around the room. "He has turned out to be as much of a perfectionist as you are."

"I'm not so much a perfectionist as just someone who likes things a certain way." Even as she said the words, LuAnn knew how silly her protest must sound, so she added a smile. "Okay, maybe I do have a teeny tiny control problem, but I'm working on it."

"No you're not, but that's okay." Tess laughed and reached across the table to pat LuAnn's arm. "I wouldn't have you change a thing, my friend. Thanks to you the inn is running like clockwork and looks absolutely gorgeous."

"It does look gorgeous, doesn't it?" LuAnn looked around the room and took note of each detail.

All the tables in the café had been decorated with small photographs in silver frames marked with discreet price stickers on the back. Larger photographs had been hung on the walls in the parlor and along the stairwell that led to the second floor. Each beautiful work of art hanging in the inn had a small card with Grant's name on it, as well as the price.

LuAnn straightened the card on the table in front of her. The photograph on this table was a shot of the inn taken a few weeks after its grand opening. Captured at sunset, the golden colors of the sky highlighted the old building and provided for a beautiful scene.

"He really has a great eye, doesn't he?"

"He's brilliant," Tess said. "But then I knew that after he did that set of portraits of the triplets. He even managed to get Henry to smile. The man is a genius."

LuAnn glanced down at her watch, and her heart lurched. "It absolutely cannot be three o'clock already." She stood and checked the time on the clock behind the desk. Indeed, that was the time.

Tess rose and picked up their coffee mugs. "I'll take care of these. You go do whatever you need to do."

The two women wandered toward the kitchen, passing the reception desk on their way. There a pair of black-and-white images of the river from last year's Sternwheel Festival competed with an enlarged portrait of the trio of retired teachers and best friends who comprised the Inn Crowd, seated on the tailgate of Tess's son's antique red pickup truck.

Taken just before last year's Marietta Fourth of July parade, the photo showed Janice smiling from the center with LuAnn and Tess on either side. The quilt that was currently draped over the inn's second-floor railing added color to the scene. In Janice's lap was a sign indicating the names of the owners of the inn.

Robin, the innkeepers' favorite female "handyperson," popped out of the office. "I like that one the best," she said. When they'd hired Robin they'd discovered she was truly a jill-of-all-trades. Today she was LuAnn's assistant.

"That was a very good day," Tess said. "Hot as blazes, even for the Fourth of July parade, but a good day all the same."

"Except for the part where the FBI showed up," LuAnn added with a shrug.

"I don't think I've heard this story," Robin said. "Why would the FBI show up at the parade?"

"Oh, you know," Tess said with a wave of her hand. "These things happen. Suffice it to say that it all worked out just fine in the end." She caught LuAnn's attention. "Just like this will. All is well. Stop worrying, Lu."

"I'm not worrying," LuAnn insisted. She hurried to straighten a frame that was tilting to the right. "Although I wish it was a little warmer today. Wouldn't it be nice to direct some of our visitors out to the patio under the stars? We could put candles on each table and offer mugs of coffee and hot chocolate."

Tess shook her head. "We can still do that. Just not in March, my friend."

LuAnn smiled. "Well, true. Unless we decide not to, we should still be participating in First Fridays once the weather is warm. Oh, I have such great plans for that area of the inn. Still, I worry about getting the flow just right. I mean, it is so lovely here inside, and just as lovely out back but—"

"What is LuAnn worrying about now?" Janice called from the second floor as she walked down the stairs toward them. "Is there another issue with the food truck?"

LuAnn froze and lifted her gaze toward Janice. "What do you mean, 'food truck'?"

She studied Tess's neutral expression, and then turned to look up again at Janice. Surely she was teasing. With Winnie out of town for a long weekend and every guest room in the inn filled, any changes to her plans were most unwelcome.

Janice had done a fabulous job of mustering the troops from her years teaching domestic arts. With her supervising and Robin acting as Janice's second-in-command, their team had turned out lunchtime soups for the café that were every bit as delicious as Winnie's. Of course, none of them would dare admit that to their intrepid chef when she returned on Monday.

LuAnn gave thanks once again for Winnie's determination to make two types of desserts and put them in the freezer in anticipation of tonight's event. Their cook had also made loaves of her fabulous sourdough bread to go along with the spreads Janice and Robin had made. With the dough rising in the kitchen, LuAnn had high hopes of success despite the fact they were using a caterer for the remainder of the food.

And speaking of caterers...

LuAnn returned her attention to Tess. "Please tell me you are just having a little fun with me. Not that it's fun, mind you, because there are a lot of last-minute details that still need to be handled. Please tell me the food is not one of them."

Robin slipped past them to reach for the mugs in Tess's hand. "I'll just go wash these and check to see how well the bread is rising," she said as she hurried to disappear into the kitchen.

Once Robin was gone, Tess rested her palms on LuAnn's shoulders and gave her a comforting look. "Lu," she said gently, "everything is fine. Just relax."

"Tess," LuAnn said as she let out a long breath. "This is me. This is our very first time to participate in First Friday."

"So you have said."

"It has to be—"

"Perfect." Tess rolled her eyes. "Yes, I know. The food is fine. Trust in your team, Lu. They know what to do. The evening will be fine."

"I know, but still. I wish Winnie were here. Then we wouldn't have to depend on a caterer."

"Well, she isn't, and that can't be helped. She'll be here next time, and you can plan something wonderful that can be eaten out on the new patio. It will be great. In the mean-time...oh!" Tess nodded toward the window. "See, look there. The food truck is parked right out front. They must be check-ing to make sure they have the correct address." Tess dropped her hands. "I'll just go say hello."

Tess hurried toward the inn's front door as Janice slipped her arm around LuAnn's waist and gave her a hug. "It's okay. Our first choice had a previous engagement. He recommended another food truck. We called, and there it is, right out front. Not only are they early, but Yelp says their lettuce cups are the best in town." She shrugged. "So it's fine."

Yelp? Since when did Janice know about Yelp?

What in the world was a lettuce cup?

And why in the world hadn't anyone thought to tell her about something as important as a change in catering? Just one thing wrong with the food, and the entire evening could be ruined.

LuAnn released the breath she hadn't realized she'd been holding. Hadn't she read in her new Bible study, *Praise before Panic,* just that morning about having faith? About allowing God to have His way with her, including letting Him have con-trol of her worries and her lists?

It was so like her to give Him advice and let Him know what worked best for each situation. However, she was learning.

"Praise before panic," she whispered as she took hold of this morning's fresh teaching. "Praise before panic."

"Yes," she said calmly. She opened her notebook and put a check beside the notation regarding food for the evening. "Thank You, Lord. It is fine. Perfectly fine. A food truck with excellent lettuce cups, it is."

The sound of tires squealing caused her to jump. Her pen clattered to the floor. A moment later Tess walked back in. "Well, that was odd."

CHAPTER TWO

W hat happened?" Janice asked as Tess walked toward them.

"It was the strangest thing," Tess said, shaking her head. "I went out to greet the food truck folks. You know, just to say hello and thank them for coming by to be sure they knew where they needed to be this evening. But before I could get there, they took off. No idea why."

"That is odd," Janice said. "But some people are always in a hurry."

"They are," Tess agreed. "At least they know where to find us for this evening."

"True." LuAnn retrieved her pen as the door opened again to reveal that Ellie Miller and Marsha Canton, two of the inn's guests, had returned.

When the two had checked in, LuAnn pegged them as the most unlikely of relatives. While Ellie was blond, cheerful, and no more than midway through her thirties, her cousin Marsha was a dour woman of middle age with dark curls. Ellie loved to talk about the wedding planning business she owned before coming to Marietta and how she hoped to continue that here, while Marsha seemed content to let her cousin have the spotlight.

In the time since the pair checked in—Apples and Cinnamon for Ellie and Moonlight and Snowflakes for Marsha—LuAnn had gotten to know Ellie fairly well over morning coffee and afternoon tea conversations, while she felt like she knew nothing of the cousin who hardly ever came out of her room to socialize. The pretty blonde's talk of the weddings she had arranged never failed to make LuAnn smile. Though Ellie had encouraged LuAnn to consider a side job helping her with the planning once her business took off, LuAnn couldn't imagine taking on more than she was already doing at the inn.

Still, it did sound like fun.

"Good afternoon, ladies," she said as she tucked the pen back into its place in the notebook. "Did you have a nice time exploring our city?"

Earlier that morning LuAnn had sent the women off with snacks from the café and a map detailing the local attractions. Ellie offered a broad smile, though her eyes seemed tired. "We did," she said. "Thank you for your assistance."

Marsha's expression was unreadable. She seemed to be scanning the room as if looking for something—or someone—to jump out and steal her cousin away.

"I saw several vacant buildings nearby that would work really well for my new shop," Ellie continued. "I can just imagine having a wedding venue downstairs and my office and catering business upstairs, plus a space for the bride and her party to get ready."

"That sounds lovely," Janice said. "Will you put in a pretty staircase for the bride and her ladies to walk down?"

"That's a must, don't you think? I would need to find a spot downstairs for the groom and his men, but that should be easy. Men don't require near as much prep space. Oh, and some of the buildings have such lovely exposed beams and brick walls. I'm going to have to call that Realtor you recommended. What was his name? Brett?"

"Brad Grimes," Janice said.

"Yes, that's right. Brad. So, anyway, with just a little paint and some imagination, I can just see the brides—"

"If you'll excuse us, I think we both need a nap," Marsha snapped, interrupting her cousin's effusive monologue.

"Be nice now," Ellie told her, seemingly unaffected by Marsha's rudeness.

"We got up early," Marsha added in a slightly kinder tone.

Ellie headed toward the framed photographs lined up on the café wall. She studied them closely, then gasped.

"These are amazing," she said over her shoulder. "Are they for sale?"

"They are," Tess said. "A local artist, Grant Grimes, is the photographer. His work will be featured tonight at our First Friday event. Anyone who attends can not only purchase his art, but also have him sign it."

"I wouldn't miss it for the world," Ellie said at the same moment that Marsha stated, "No, we have plans."

"Plans to meet the man who took this one," Ellie said, ignoring Marsha to gesture to a picture of the river with a couple seated on a bench in the distance. "This will look absolutely perfect above the mantel in my new home. Would you mind setting it aside for me?"

LuAnn placed her notebook on the nearest table and joined Ellie. "That's the same one I have on my nightstand," she said. "Grant gave me a print of it last month."

Ellie looked dismayed. "Do you think there are many more prints of it around? Usually I try to purchase prints that aren't mass produced."

"I don't think there are very many," LuAnn said. "I don't have any sold tags out yet, but I can pull this one and put it in our office. You can pick it up there this evening and have Grant sign it then. He should be arriving around five thirty."

"Perfect," Ellie said as she grinned at Marsha. "Now, I believe it's nap time. See you all at five thirty."

Tess watched the pair make their way upstairs. Once the doors to their rooms had closed behind them, she shook her head. "There is something off about those two. Don't you think?"

LuAnn shrugged. "Right now I can't think about anything other than making sure tonight goes just right."

Tess's attention returned to LuAnn and then to Janice. "But you see it, right? Ellie is so bubbly and fun, and Marsha is so . . ."

"So not?" Janice supplied.

"Exactly," Tess said with a shrug. "Of course, opposites do attract in friendships as in families. Look at us."

"What do you mean?" Janice asked. "I think we three are very much alike. I mean, we're all retired teachers, we all agreed to be partners here at the inn, and we certainly all love Jesus."

The door opened, and a large vase of flowers with legs stepped inside. "Flowers are here," the delivery woman said as she peered around the colorful mass of perennials.

"Oh, they're beautiful," Tess exclaimed. "Here, put them on the…" She paused to look over at LuAnn. "Where would you like them?"

LuAnn knew exactly where the plan in her notebook intended the vase to go. However, this was her moment to give up control. Her opportunity to become the new, laid-back LuAnn.

Thus, she pasted on a smile. "Wherever you think best," she told Tess.

"If you're sure." Tess nodded to the florist. "Over here on the desk would be great."

"I'm going to go check on the…" LuAnn paused as the florist headed for the front desk. "You know," she said before she could stop herself, "why don't you set that vase over on the piano? I think it would look really lovely there. The little bud vases with white roses will go one to each table over in the café, and there should be a few other smaller arrangements that match the larger one. Just put them all on the front desk and I will place them when I get a chance."

Tess met her gaze with a smile that quickly became a chuckle once the florist had disappeared outside. "For a minute I wondered what you had done with my friend."

LuAnn's shoulders sank. "I'm awful," she said. "But I am working on it."

"You are a treasure," Janice replied. "What would we do without your organizational skills?"

"Put the flowers in the wrong place," Tess said with a wink.

LuAnn shook her head. "It's that new Bible study we started yesterday. After reading the first chapter, I'm feeling convicted over some issues I have with control."

Janice clasped LuAnn's hand. "Please don't be convicted to change that part of your personality until after the First Friday event is over. We need you to make sure everything is done the way it should be."

"I agree," Tess said. "Although I might have worded it a little more subtly."

"Oh, you know what I mean," Janice protested. "I didn't say it right, but I am always so impressed at how you can pull things off like this event tonight with what seems like little or no effort. You're really good at it, so maybe the Lord gave you that skill for a reason. Don't toss it away too quickly."

"Perhaps you're right," LuAnn said. "But I'm not sure I have a good grasp on—"

Her phone rang, and she glanced down to see that Brad was calling. Instantly, she smiled. What was it about the town's favorite Realtor that always brought a grin to her face?

"Sorry. I need to take this. Can we talk more later? I really do want to figure out what God wants me to do about this."

"Count on it," Tess said. "But I'm going on the record as the inn's business manager saying I don't want to lose my best list maker."

"We'll see what God says about that." LuAnn grinned and took a step away to answer the phone.

"I thought I would check and see if you need any help with putting things together for the event," Brad said. "I know Grant will be there around five thirty, but I thought I might be able to come earlier. Say, five. Or sooner if you need me."

"That's sweet of you," she said as she glanced around the nearly completed space. There wasn't a thing Brad could do that hadn't already been done. And yet, her smile grew. "Five would be great. Thank you for offering."

"Oh, and there's one more thing," he said. "A client of mine would like an introduction to the owners of the famous Wayfarers Inn. I told her I would see if I could arrange that."

"So the inn is famous now. I like hearing that."

"It is." He chuckled. "I'm not saying she won't buy the house I showed her if I don't accomplish this meeting, but she really seemed interested in speaking with you."

"Of course," LuAnn said. "Although I cannot imagine what she would want to talk to us about. Is she considering becoming an innkeeper?"

"Actually, Marissa Endicott is the new reporter for the local paper. I think she's looking to interview you as part of an article she's working on about First Friday. I think you'll like her."

"Why would you think that?" As soon as LuAnn realized she'd said it out loud, she cringed. She spied Janice and Tess watching her and turned away from them so they couldn't see her face. "Sorry, that was a dumb question. I'm sure I will."

"She's great," he quickly assured her. "She's smart and funny and has great taste in houses. We've had a great time looking for the right property for her."

"I'm sure you have," she muttered, suddenly irritated.

"Are you all right?" Brad asked.

"Yes, fine. Just distracted." LuAnn shifted positions to look in the direction of the café. "Please tell Marissa we would be happy to speak with her."

"I'll let you tell her yourself," he said. "That is if you don't mind that I bring her with me."

"No." But she did mind. The feeling was completely unexpected and unwelcome.

"No?" he asked.

LuAnn shook her head. "I meant no, I don't mind."

"Okay, great. See you at five o'clock, then. You're going to love Marissa."

LuAnn said goodbye and hung up before she could say anything that would make her cringe. What was wrong with her? Despite what her two best friends thought, there was no indication of a relationship brewing between her and Brad other than friendship. Jealousy certainly had no place there.

So if he wanted to bring a reporter named Marissa Endicott with him to the inn, then so be it. And if that reporter made him happy, then she would do as the Bible said and rejoice with his rejoicing.

LuAnn turned around to see Tess and Janice still watching her closely. "What?" she asked.

Tess's brows rose. "Seems like something has you upset, that's all."

"Not at all," she managed. "I was just thinking about rejoicing with my friend's rejoicing..." LuAnn shook her head. "Or something like that. It's biblical," she said lamely.

"Well, I'm glad Brad didn't say something to make you upset." Janice hurried to explain. "I was standing right there when your phone rang. I couldn't help seeing that Brad was the caller."

"You are right and wrong," LuAnn said as she tucked her phone back into her pocket. She offered her best friends a smile. "It was Brad, but I am not upset. In fact, I have good news. One of his clients just happens to be a reporter for the local paper, and she's doing a piece on First Friday. He's bringing her to meet us."

"So that's why you're rejoicing?" Janice asked.

Tess elbowed Janice. "And that is also why she's frowning."

"I am not frowning," LuAnn said. "And now if you will excuse me, I'm going to go check on things in the kitchen."

"Things in the kitchen are fine," Janice said. "Robin is working on the bread, and my high school girls will be here in an hour to start preparing the desserts and appetizers."

"And the food truck now knows how to find us," Tess said with a shrug. "So how old is this reporter friend of Brad's? And is she single?"

LuAnn's temper flared. "I have no idea," she said. "And I didn't ask."

"Honey," Janice said gently, "is there more to this than you're telling us?"

"No," LuAnn said, calming. "Brad is showing houses to a new reporter for the local paper. She's doing a piece on First Friday, and she wants to include us. And that's all. Besides the fact she's smart and funny and they're having a wonderful time looking for the perfect home for her, and oh my. What am I doing? This is ridiculous." She shook her head. "I am officially out of my mind. Our friend Brad is doing us a favor, and I've turned it into something to be upset about. Now…" She took a deep breath and let it out slowly. "I am going to review my checklist one more time. Once that is done, I plan to call Grant and have him finalize the photographs he wants to exhibit. Then, I will go upstairs and get ready for the evening. Unless either of you know of anything else I need to do," she added.

"Not me," Janice said.

"Nope," Tess answered.

Completing the tasks left on her list didn't take long. She wandered into the kitchen, following her nose and the scent of baking sourdough bread. Janice must have anticipated her visit, because she had a freshly cut slice of bread with butter and a knife waiting beside it, and a mug set out next to the coffeepot.

The moment the kitchen door closed behind her, LuAnn's tension melted away. Though evidence of tonight's food littered the counters, the mess did not distract her from the smile the room put on her face.

LuAnn poured a mug of coffee, sweetened it, and then took a slice of bread covered in creamy butter over to the kitchen island to seat herself on one of the barstools. Janice had followed her and now stood in front of Big Red, the massive 1950s-era stove painted fire engine red, stirring something.

"Have you finished everything?" Janice asked as she turned down the heat on the burner and set the spoon on the apple-shaped spoon rest.

Though tempted to say she still had plenty of details to go back and check, LuAnn took a sip of coffee and nodded. "I've crossed everything off my list except a call to Grant to see if he has any more changes to the photos he wants to showcase."

"But you're putting that off?"

"I am. I figure if I wait until the last minute, I'll get the last version. If that makes sense."

"It does." Janice wiped her hands on the dish towel and set it aside to join LuAnn at the kitchen island. "Speaking of the Grimes brothers."

"Were we?" LuAnn asked. "I thought we were only speaking of the Grimes brother. Singular, not plural."

Janice grinned. "Okay, so I didn't transition well. Speaking of *Brad*," she said, "I couldn't help but notice you were a little miffed during your phone call with him. I know you explained why but, as your friend, can I ask you something very personal?"

LuAnn took another sip of coffee and allowed the warm liquid to slide down her throat. She knew what was coming and wanted to have nothing to do with the conversation Janice apparently wished to have. But… "You can ask me anything," she said.

"Okay," Janice said slowly. "I know you've told Tess and me that you don't want to discuss any kind of romantic relationship with Brad."

"Because there isn't one," she said. "We're just friends."

"I understand, and I think that's great." Janice fussed with a napkin and looked back up at LuAnn. "I just don't want you to miss any signs that Brad might be the man for you because you're so focused on just being his friend."

"Is that what you think I'm doing?" LuAnn asked.

Janice shrugged. "I don't know. Probably not. I'm a terrible one to talk to about friendships turning to romance and getting married. I only did it once, and that was a long time ago."

They shared a chuckle. Then Janice's expression sobered. "Just keep an open mind about what God has for you."

"With Brad?" LuAnn asked.

"Not specifically," Janice said. "I told you I'm terrible at this. If you and Brad are meant to just be friends, then great. He's my friend too, and I like him a lot. But if there's something more that's meant to be, whether it's with Brad or someone else, I don't want you to miss out."

"Why do you think I might miss out? Is it because I've been single all my life?"

Janice inhaled deeply, then let out a long breath. "Not necessarily. The Lord calls some to marriage and some to singleness. If we're called to one of those, then how can we think we're missing out on the other?"

"Right," LuAnn said. "So what is it, then?"

"It's something you said earlier about control." She shrugged. "I'm just a former pastor's wife who is trying to figure out what comes next for me, so please don't take my words as anything other than the loving rambles of a friend."

"Always," LuAnn said warmly.

"I've been thinking about what you said about how our Bible study has convicted you with some issues you have with control." Janice paused to trace the edge of the countertop. "Being in a relationship is the ultimate loss of control. It becomes less about you and more about the two of you. Does that frighten you?"

And there it was. Her worst fear laid bare right here in the kitchen with her best friend sitting across from her.

"I was in a relationship twice, you know," LuAnn managed, hoping she did not sound as if she was going on the defensive. Those losses were well behind her, and yet the painful lessons she had learned were as fresh as if they had happened yesterday or the day before.

"You were," Janice said.

"And perhaps I will be again," LuAnn said with a smile. "But not now."

Janice nodded and stretched her hand across the divide between them. "That is a very good answer, my friend."

LuAnn grinned. "I thought so too."

Now to make herself believe it.

CHAPTER THREE

LuAnn washed out her mug and plate and put them on the rack to dry. Wiping her hands on the dish towel, she stared out the window at the beautiful blue sky. Wisps of feathery clouds floated by on the spring breeze. In a few months, a sunny day would mean people out biking or hiking, or perhaps renting a kayak and taking to the river.

Today it meant standing at the sink and wishing. She smiled to herself.

"Thank you," she said over her shoulder at Janice, who was now back at the stove stirring.

"Any time," she said. "You know where to find me."

LuAnn laughed. "That's true. Now, I'm going to make that call and then go soak in a tub of lavender bubbles until I absolutely must get ready."

She tucked the phone into her pocket and headed upstairs to the apartments on the top floor. The rooms included a common sitting area and small kitchen as well as a bedroom, sitting room, and bath for each of the three owners.

As usual, Huck and Tom met her at the door to the common room. Between the enthusiastic pup's excited leaping and the kitty rubbing circles around her ankles, she had to wade her way over to the seating area.

LuAnn settled onto the chair by the window, where Huck immediately jumped into her lap and Tom landed at his side. While the inn's pets vied for position on her lap, she dialed Grant's number. He picked up on the second ring with a cheery greeting.

"I'm glad you called, LuAnn," he said. "I was just thinking about making some changes to the show. See, I didn't tell you this before, but I've been experimenting with this antique camera I found a few months ago, and I've got a few tintypes ready for the show. What do you think?"

"I think you've lost your mind," she said with a giggle. "And I also think you're teasing me."

He joined her in laughter. "Okay, I am teasing, in part. I don't plan on making any changes to the photographs I want to show tonight. However, I actually did find an old camera, circa 1860 or so, and I am learning how to use it, so that's pretty cool."

"Oh, wow, it is," she said. "Maybe we'll showcase your tintypes next time."

"Let's see if I can figure out how to make them first."

"All right, that's fair." She paused. "Hey, congratulations though. You've already made a sale. One of our guests bought the photograph of the couple down by the river."

"That's great," he said. "The same one you have?"

"The very same," she said. "Except, of course, mine is smaller. So either bring another print, or I'll fill in with another photograph. Your choice. Either way, I must get ready, so I'll see you at five thirty."

"Yes ma'am," he told her. "And LuAnn? Thank you for this opportunity. I've never shown my photographs before, other than to friends and relatives and other captive audiences."

She laughed. "I wish you'd have let me pay for the one you gave me."

"No way," he said. "But I'll gladly let other people. I'll call before I leave to see if you need me to bring anything else."

"Okay, great," she said as she patted Huck's head and then did the same for Tom. "See you in a bit."

LuAnn said goodbye and tucked the phone back into her pocket. "All right, kids," she said to the pets. "Time to move."

Huck jumped off her lap immediately, wagging his tail. Tom, however, merely gave her a lazy look and then closed his eyes.

"Well then," LuAnn told the cat. She picked him up, then set him gently back on the empty chair after she stood. "You'll just have to nap here without me."

She wandered into her room with Huck on her heels, then paused to see if Tom planned to follow. When there was no response from the kitty other than a stretch and a yawn, she closed the door behind her. Though she had been living here far too long to call it a new place, she still felt that rush of a thrill every time she stepped into her own space.

"Thank You, Lord," she whispered as she pulled the phone out of her pocket and set it on the nightstand beside the photo she had received from Grant. Huck made himself at home in his bed.

She reached for the photograph, curling her fingers around the intricate silver frame. Though the print for sale downstairs was much bigger—sixteen by twenty inches—this one was just right for her nightstand at a smaller eight by ten inches.

It was also the perfect size to hide her most prized possessions.

Lowering herself to the edge of her bed, LuAnn turned the frame over and pried open the back. There, hidden behind the photo, was a letter that had turned brown around the edges along with an old picture.

She placed the letter on the quilt and turned the photograph over to reveal two smiling faces. One belonged to her, and the other was her father.

She traced the edge of the photo with her fingertip as her attention went from the little girl with the blond hair to the man whose face she could only recall because it had been captured here in this picture. Though she knew now why her father disappeared from her life without a trace, that knowledge did not make up for the loss she still felt.

LuAnn wondered what her life might have been like if her father hadn't been a hero. If he hadn't testified against those men. If he hadn't chosen to keep her and Mama safe by going into the witness protection program without so much as a hint of it to his family.

The sound of footsteps coming up the stairs caused her to return the photograph and letter to the frame. Huck lifted his head as if to investigate, and then lowered it again. Though the footsteps continued on, likely Tess heading toward her rooms, LuAnn returned the photograph to her nightstand.

There was something comforting about having those last two remaining pieces of her father's memory nearby and hidden from everyone but herself. Her father had died a decade or more ago, and the chance to know him had died with him.

She moved past the nightstand and into the attached bathroom, where she ran hot water in the tub and then added a generous amount of lavender-scented bath salts. She had always enjoyed taking a long soak at the end of her workday during the years when she taught.

The only thing that got her out of the water was the clock. She now had just enough time to dress and let Huck out for his business before Brad was due to arrive. Brad and Marissa, she reminded herself, and this time she felt no twinge of whatever it was that had plagued her before.

Instead, she could rejoice that Brad was bringing a friend who just might become her friend too. And if not a friend, then at least someone who would mention the inn in a favorable light in the local paper.

"See there?" she said. "I can rejoice, Lord. Just watch me."

May 1, 1860

Chaos reigned in the city as Prudence clutched tightly to Jason with one hand and cradled Moses with the other. Even those who had not seen the light streak across the sky had come to investigate after feeling the rumble underfoot. Truly she had not seen so many people thronging the streets since that awful night almost a year ago when the fires chased people from their homes.

Jason nodded toward a group of a dozen or so friends from church, and they headed in that direction. While he joined the men, Prudence was happy to find company with the women. Of course, the matter up for discussion was which of the ladies would capture Moses's attention first.

Moses settled the debate by slipping from her arms to toddle toward his father, who caught him and nodded at Prudence with a smile.

The women were now chattering about this afternoon's event, each talking over the other until the words were scattered and lost. "Fire from the sky, it was," one said. "A streak longer than a mile and whistling like my old grandfather used to," another claimed.

Prudence looked past them to where Jason was listening intently. Moses was now content to rest his head on his father's shoulder, likely tuckered out from all the wiggling he did on their walk here. A stranger had joined them, a man who looked to be doing all the talking while the others merely listened in silence or nodded at intervals.

After a moment, Jason caught her attention. She excused herself to join him as he stepped away from the men.

"What has thee learned?" she asked him. "Has war come to Marietta?"

"The fire in the sky was not likely from an enemy," Jason said. "Although no one has determined as yet where it did come from. All that is known is that something streaked across the sky. It either was due to or caused by an earthquake. Men from the college are gathering now to go out and see if they can find the source."

"What source?" she said.

Jason shrugged. "The theory among the men at the college is that the object we saw might have been a meteorite. That is what I prefer to believe. The alternative is that war has indeed come and with it some invention that allows the enemy to shoot from a long distance."

"I do hope the men from the college are right."

"As do I, but in any case there seems no need to remain in Marietta today except to stand in the street. Perhaps we return another day to complete our errands?"

"Agreed."

They wove a path through the citizens now milling about on the main street. By holding on to Jason's sleeve, Prudence kept up with his pace until they reached the edge of the city. There he stopped, and they turned back to look at the town.

"Even if the men from the college are right, is there cause for concern?" Prudence asked.

"No more than on any other day," he said.

His words followed her back along the river to their home. Moses slept on his father's shoulder, and then remained asleep when Jason lowered him onto the cot beside their bed. They stepped outside to sit on the porch together.

For a while they sat in silence, and then Jason turned to face Prudence. "The man from the college asked for help in locating pieces of the thing that fell from the sky."

"Oh?" she said as she reached down to Patience to silence her honking.

"I have volunteered."

"You?" she said, and then wished she could take the question back.

Ever since Jason's injury while working with his fellow members of the Underground Railroad before they married, he had never been able to keep up with an able-bodied man's swift pace. His leg pains were a source of occasional trouble, but truly Prudence never thought him any less of a man because of them.

However, to take on a strenuous hike to who knew where? And to volunteer for a search that could prove dangerous if the theory of the falling meteorite turned out to be wrong?

She opened her mouth to speak, and then her eyes met his. Her heart lurched. This man wanted to take on a role in the search. Truly wanted to do it. One word from her, however, and he would not.

And so she made the difficult choice to turn her fears to God and her smile toward her husband. "When will thee go, then?"

"Now, if I am not to be left behind," he told her.

She nodded. "Do I have time to pack thee something to eat?"

A broad grin lit his face. "Indeed," he told her. "And perhaps a double helping of thy cornbread should one of my fellow searchers not be so blessed as to have a wife who can cook as thee can?"

Prudence climbed to her feet, and then leaned down to kiss her husband on the forehead. "Or a triple helping so that thee might have double?"

He laughed. "Indeed thee is a smart woman."

A short while later, Jason bid her goodbye and left her standing on the porch to watch him go. "Perhaps Moses and I could go with you as far as Marietta," she called. "What does thee say?"

"Stay home, Prudence." He turned around to face her. "See to our son, and wait for my return. And promise me not to worry."

"I cannot," she said.

"Then promise me to trust that the Lord will not let me go where He does not go along with me. The man at the college is not blind. He saw I am not fully capable of what others can do. Still he said he can make use of my help. And so I will help."

"Yes," she said. "I understand."

"See to Moses," he said, and then blew her a kiss. "And I will have a promise from thee that there will be no helping the railroad while I am away. I will make it known thee is unavailable for a time."

"But what if…" She closed her mouth to words she ought not say. "Yes, Husband," she said as he turned back toward the trail. "I promise."

How many times had he watched her walk off on a mission for the Underground Railroad that gave him cause to wonder if he might not see her return? And here she was, fighting tears because her husband was going to look for fallen rocks with the men from the college.

What was wrong with her?

She heard Moses whimper. Soon his tears would join hers, and he would want comfort. Prudence turned to follow the sound of her son's cry. While there was no comfort for her until her husband returned, at least she could make her son smile.

"Come, Patience," she called to the white goose. "Moses is awake and fussing."

Though the bird knew not to enter the farmhouse, she was happy waiting at the door. A moment later, Prudence lifted Moses off the cot and carried him into the other room where the goose in the doorway was clearly visible to the still-sleepy little boy.

In an instant, Moses let out a squeal, his chubby legs kicking at the air until Prudence finally set him on his feet. The moment his toes touched the floor, he was off toward

Patience who offered a happy series of honks, and the game they both enjoyed was on.

The goose was not only faster, but she was also smarter and louder. Thus, Patience was never caught. Instead, Moses ran and played until his little legs could carry him no more. Finally he climbed the steps to settle into Prudence's lap.

As she nestled him against her, she thought of Jason making his way toward Marietta, and tears once again threatened to spill. A tug at her skirt distracted her, and Prudence looked down to find Patience beside her. "Is thee trying to keep me from my tears now?"

Patience gave her a look that said she wanted to play. And then she honked.

CHAPTER FOUR

Frue to his word, Brad arrived at exactly five o'clock. However, he was alone.

"Marissa will be here later," he said as he glanced around the room. "The paper arranged another interview at the last minute, so she had to go there first. Wow, this place looks great."

"LuAnn did it all," Tess said as she walked out of the office to stand at the front desk.

"Nonsense," she said. "I had plenty of help."

"Speaking of help, what can I do?"

Janice popped her head out of the kitchen. "You can help in here," she called. "We're up to our eyeballs in cooking and need someone to do the stirring while we finish up."

"I'm your man," Brad said. He smiled at Tess and LuAnn before following Janice back into the kitchen.

When the door closed behind Brad, LuAnn turned back to Tess and found her frowning. "What?"

"Nothing," Tess said. "Is there anything on your list that still needs doing?"

"It's all done," she said. "We are ready for our guests." LuAnn frowned. "Wait. The food truck?"

Tess shook her head. "That's an interesting story. I got a call a few minutes ago from the owner of the food truck. They're almost here. I told him where to park."

"Good," LuAnn said. "I'm counting on those lettuce cups to live up to their Yelp reviews."

"I'm sure they will." Tess paused. "But there's more. I asked him why he left in such a hurry earlier."

"What did he say?"

"That he wasn't here earlier. He said he was working a lunch shift over at the college until an hour ago." She shrugged. "I wish I had paid more attention to the name on that truck. Did you happen to notice?"

"I didn't," LuAnn said. "I wonder if Janice did."

Tess nodded toward the kitchen door. "Do you want to go ask her, or should I?"

LuAnn's phone rang, and she smiled. "Saved by the bell. It's Thorn. Why don't you watch for the food truck and speak to the owner when they get here? I'll handle this call from Thorn and then check with Janice."

"Okay," Tess said. "And this time I'll make note of the name on the truck."

"Good idea," LuAnn said, then answered her phone to greet her friend and the inn's best handyman.

"I know you're busy," he said, "but I have a favor to ask."

"Sure, name it," she said. She cradled the phone between her shoulder and ear so she could straighten a photograph that wasn't hanging quite right.

"Well, I'm coming to the First Friday event tonight."

"Great," she said.

"And I'm bringing a friend with me." He paused. "A date."

That got her attention. "Oh?"

"Yeah," he said slowly. "Beverly."

Tory "Thorn" Thornton and Beverly were married when they were barely out of their teens. War and stupidity on his part had separated them and ultimately caused their divorce. At least that's how Thorn told the story. The marriage had produced a daughter, Laura, with whom he was now becoming reacquainted here in Marietta. The added bonus of that reunion was that Beverly had returned also, and the two of them were getting to know one another again.

"That's wonderful, Thorn," she said. "I'm very happy for both of you."

"There's not much to be happy for just yet. I owe that woman more apologies than I could give her if I lived another hundred years, but I thought I can at least start saying them, you know?"

"I do," she said. "So what's the favor? Name it."

"I appreciate that, LuAnn. I'm a little nervous about this. I haven't been on a date in a very long time, so I need to practice what I ought to do."

"I'm not sure I understand," she said slowly. "You want advice on how to date? Don't you think you want to ask a guy that? I don't know anything about it from a man's point of view."

"Oh no," he said quickly. "I just need some advice on what I ought to wear. I'm back at the loading dock right now, and I can't decide which tie works with my suit or whether I ought to wear a suit at all or just stick with a shirt and tie."

She grinned. "I'll be right there."

LuAnn tucked her phone into her sweater pocket and hurried to the loading dock where she found Thorn waiting. From his sheepish expression to his dark suit and royal-blue tie, he looked every bit like an over-forty prom date.

"Well?" he said warily as he held both arms out. "What do you think?"

She smiled. "Show me the other tie."

He reached into his pocket and unrolled a black tie, and then held it out toward her. LuAnn shook her head. "Nope. Wear the blue one tonight."

"Thanks." He smiled. "Wish me luck."

"I'll do even better than that," she said. "I'll pray."

His smile broadened as he nodded and turned to leave. Before returning to the reception, LuAnn made a detour to her room to retrieve her digital camera from her desk. She was determined to get some good shots of their first First Friday for their website.

By the time LuAnn returned to the lobby area, Grant had arrived a bit early with his daughter Saffron in tow. To LuAnn's surprise, he had ditched his usual Hawaiian shirt and jeans for a more dressed-up pair of slacks and a sweater. His only nod to his favorite island-themed attire was the pineapple logo on his sweater. LuAnn got a great father/daughter shot of the two of them.

While Grant arranged things at the spot where he would be signing, Saffron wandered over to the wall by the staircase to study the photographs. "He's really good," she said to LuAnn when she came to stand beside her.

"He is," LuAnn said. "Did you see the one he did of you and your sister? It's up on the stairs to the right. You can't miss it."

Saffron grinned and headed for the stairs as the inn's doors opened and a group of visitors wandered inside, their first First Friday guests. Marietta fireman Justin O'Hara paused in the doorway. LuAnn couldn't help but notice his attention was focused on the stairs where Saffron stood.

"Hello, Justin," LuAnn called. "Welcome to the inn. Are you here for First Friday?"

"Actually, I was here to see if your fire permits were up-to-date." At LuAnn's likely horrified expression, he hurried to continue. "I'm just kidding. I came to let Mr. Grimes know I'm ready to list that little house on Cherry Street for rent."

"You could have come to the office in the morning, but hey, that's great news." Grant reached out to shake Justin's hand. "If you're ready, I'll start showing it. I'll email you the listing agreement tonight so you can look it over."

"That sounds good." The men shook hands, then Justin turned back to LuAnn. "So, I've got a picture in mind to buy, but it looks like I have a competitor for my bid."

LuAnn grinned as the door opened again, this time admitting at least a dozen folks. "Why don't you go up and see if you can strike a deal?"

Justin set off toward the stairs. When LuAnn returned her attention to Grant, she found that he was now staring up at his daughter and the fireman. Though several people were also standing on the stairs, the two seemed oblivious to anything but each other.

"Grant," LuAnn said gently, "you're staring with an expression that is less than welcoming. That's rude, don't you think?"

"That's being a father," he said. "Have I missed something? Are those two an item? He's too old for Saffron."

"They're the same age, and as far as I know, not yet," she told him. "But it looks like Justin is trying to remedy that."

"Oh no, he isn't." Grant shook his head. "No man who's appeared on a fireman's pinup calendar is going to date my daughter."

"It was for a good cause." LuAnn chuckled. "He also appeared in newspapers all over the place honoring him for saving my best friend and business partner, so there's that."

Grant sighed. "He did, didn't he?"

"Yes," she said. She patted his arm. "He did. So if anyone is going to date your daughter, wouldn't you prefer him to be hero material?"

He returned his attention to LuAnn. "Anyone is better than that fool she was going out with for so long. I never understood a man who would rather research a rare species of mussels than spend time with my daughter." He shook his head. "You know, I don't have anything against Justin, per se. He's a good man, hardworking, and, as you said, he's a hero. It's just difficult to see a guy paying attention to my daughter."

"That is a perfectly normal reaction."

LuAnn nodded toward Tess who had returned bearing plates filled with something that looked like individual small spears of lettuce with different fillings inside. The effect was brilliant: a salad you could pick up and eat while gazing at art. Or buying it.

"It looks like the food has arrived," she told Grant. "Why don't you fix yourself a plate?"

He shook his head. "I couldn't eat. Too nervous."

"Why's that?" She snatched a blue cheese and steak lettuce cup off the tray as Tess breezed past. "Your work is amazing. You've already sold one piece, so you know you'll have sales. Just relax. Have a lettuce cup." She took a bite. "Oh, definitely have a lettuce cup. Yelp was right. They're amazing."

"Maybe later. So who bought my photo?"

"Her name is Ellie, and she's a guest here. A wedding planner relocating to Marietta. Brad's working with her. I'll introduce you when she comes downstairs." The door opened again. "Oh, I have to welcome more guests. This is going to be great, Grant. I just know it."

"In case you're busy, how will I know this woman? I want to be sure I properly thank her for her purchase. It's my first sale ever, and I would like her to know I appreciate it."

"Trust me," she said. "You'll know. Suffice it to say that when Ellie arrives, you and every other man in the room will know it."

He chuckled. "Really?"

"Really." LuAnn glanced up at the clock and saw that it was exactly five thirty. She returned her attention to Grant. "She should be coming down here any minute. Just watch the stairs."

It was closer to seven when Ellie made her debut, but she arrived with such flair that no one could have missed her. A quick look over at Grant, who until that moment had been busy signing a photo for Margaret Ashworth, told LuAnn he had certainly noticed.

She spied Janice and Tess also watching. While Janice met LuAnn's gaze and grinned, Tess never removed her attention from Ellie.

Pastor Ben Murphey and his heavily pregnant wife, Paige, stepped inside the front doors, and LuAnn hurried to greet them.

"Looks like the party is in full swing," Pastor Ben said with a smile. "Half the town must be here."

Indeed, the room was filled to capacity with friends, family, and folks LuAnn had never met. She kept busy snapping photo after photo of their guests. Over in the corner, huddled together in front of a photograph of the inn, stood Thorn and Beverly. The previously nervous handyman now wore a look of happiness that could be felt even at this distance. His beautiful red-haired ex-wife matched him in her expression while their daughter, Laura, looked on with her husband Jake at her side. LuAnn lifted her gaze upward in thanks for what she hoped was an answer to prayer.

She returned her attention to Pastor Ben and Paige, now standing beside her. "Come in and shop," she told them. "Or just enjoy the food."

Paige grinned. "I believe I'll do both."

The couple headed toward the table where Winnie's treats mingled with the delicious food from the truck now parked discreetly behind the building. LuAnn returned her attention to the grand entrance their wedding planner guest was making.

As Ellie moved closer, parting the crowd of shoppers milling about like a knife through warm butter, Grant rose and smiled at her. LuAnn could see that he was smitten.

And, it appeared, so was Ellie. She made her way across the room slowly, yet purposefully, looking neither to the left nor to the right.

"I'm terribly sorry I'm late," she said, not looking the least bit repentant. Her gaze fell to the camera in LuAnn's hand, and her eyes widened. "Are you taking pictures tonight?"

LuAnn smiled at her. "Yes, I'm trying to get some good candid shots to post on our website. Hopefully that'll bring even more people to the inn next month."

Ellie turned from her and looked expectantly at Grant.

LuAnn took the hint. "Ellie Miller," she said, "this is Grant Grimes, our guest photographer. And Grant, I would like you to meet the very first person to purchase one of your photographs, Miss Ellie Miller."

"Ellie," he said as he extended his hand to her in greeting, "it is truly an honor."

"The honor is mine," Ellie responded in a silky voice. "I had no idea that the man who took such beautiful pictures would be so handsome." She gave him a sweeping glance, then returned her attention to his face.

Grant seemed unable to speak, so LuAnn stepped in to save him. "Where is your cousin tonight, Ellie? I thought you two were inseparable."

Ellie's smile wavered, but only for a moment. "Oh, I'm sure she'll be along soon. These artsy things aren't things she enjoys. She was raised in the country and just didn't have the privileges I had, so she hasn't learned to appreciate the finer things."

"Well, I have," Grant said. "And I am looking at one right now."

Maybelline looked beyond the pair to catch LuAnn's attention and rolled her eyes. LuAnn merely grinned.

So intent was LuAnn on watching love bloom between Grant and Ellie, she never noticed Thorn, dropping down on one knee right there in front of half the town.

"Marry me, Bev," he declared loudly enough to silence the room. "Let's run off right now and make this legal."

CHAPTER FIVE

Y ou'll do nothing of the sort," Laura exclaimed. "Doing this right should mean having a wedding. My mother deserves her moment, and Jake and I will see that she gets it."

Tess and Janice moved over to join LuAnn for a better view. "Can you believe this is happening?" Tess whispered to them.

"I'm just so glad it's happening," LuAnn said.

"Really, Laura," Bev said as she looked down at Thorn and then back up. "It's fine."

"It is not fine," Laura insisted, turning toward her father. "The first time you and Mom got married, you did the justice of the peace thing. Don't you think my mother will make a beautiful bride? In a wedding dress? Don't you think she deserves that? On a day where you two commit to each other before God and your friends?"

Thorn seemed to consider these questions as the room fell silent. "I do see your point," he finally said, then returned his attention to Bev. "I say let the girl throw us a wedding. What do you think, sweetheart?"

Bev nodded, tears shimmering in her eyes. "I would like that. But first, I wonder if your knees are going to let you stand up on your own, or if we're going to have to help you."

"I think I can do it, but I don't intend to do this again, just for the record."

"Well, just for the record," she said as she patted his arm, "I don't intend to give you cause for doing this again."

Thorn's face softened. "Nor do I, sweetheart."

He climbed to his feet and turned to Laura. "There, see? I did it. Now then, you make your plans, but I've got just one condition."

"What's that?" Laura asked.

"At our age, your mama and I won't be having a long engagement. If you can't get us hitched by the end of the month, come April Fools' Day, we're heading for City Hall. Understand?"

"Mom," Laura said, "you can't possibly agree with him."

Bev's grin broadened as she embraced her former and future husband. "I'd say the end of the month is about as long as I'm willing to wait for the honeymoon."

"Don't you mean the wedding?" Laura asked.

"Trust me," Tess said as she joined them. "I'm sure your mom said what she meant. So where will this wedding happen?"

"We could host the wedding here," Janice offered. "I wouldn't mind playing the 'Bridal Chorus' on the piano as Bev comes down the staircase."

"That sounds lovely," Bev said. "But we couldn't impose."

"We insist," Tess said as LuAnn nodded.

"A wedding. How fun!" Ellie said as she strolled toward them, with Grant following in her wake. "I don't have a business card handy, but I was a highly sought after wedding planner back home. I hadn't intended to get back to work here in Marietta until I was settled in, but what better time than now to offer my services? Let me plan your wedding."

LuAnn glanced around to see if the owners of Tie the Knot, the local Marietta wedding planning service, were in attendance to hear this exclamation. From her vantage point, she did not see them.

Laura hesitated. "We can't pay much."

"Don't you worry about a thing," Ellie said. She patted Laura's shoulder. "My services will be on the house. All I'll want from you is an endorsement to help me get established in town."

"Surely we can pay you something for your expertise," Thorn said.

"Well," she said sweetly, as she latched onto Grant's arm and beamed up at him, "I wouldn't mind if someone wanted to buy me one or two of this guy's photographs."

"Absolutely," Laura said. "Name your price, Grant."

Rather than look over at Laura, Grant's focus remained on Ellie. "You've got a deal, and Laura won't owe me a cent. My payment will be allowing me to photograph you. I've got this new camera, and I would love to see what you look like in tin."

Her smile fell. "Tin?"

LuAnn stepped in. "He bought an antique camera recently. The photographs are done the nineteenth-century way, on pieces of tin."

"Oh well, in that case, Mr. Grimes," Ellie said sweetly, "you've got yourself a deal." She tore her attention away from

Grant to smile at the bride and groom. "And you two have got yourself a March wedding."

"And a preacher to perform that wedding," Pastor Ben said. "As long as Paige doesn't decide to have our little one the same day."

"I'm sure that won't happen," Paige told the happy couple as she patted her expansive middle. "My obstetrician says I'm not due until March twenty-fourth, but I am absolutely certain that Baby Murphey will come any day now."

"Then I say we have the wedding on the sixteenth." Thorn turned to Bev. "What do you say, honey?"

Bev beamed up at him. "I think I can wait two weeks to be married to you." Her expression sobered. "But that doesn't give much time for planning, not that we want anything fancy. And we truly do not want to have our wedding interrupt family time with a new baby."

"No, really," Paige said. "I believe our little one will be coming any time now."

Bev gave her a look of concern. "Are you having contractions?"

"No, but my doctor told me the best way to bring on labor is to walk."

"So she's walking," Ben said. "A lot. All the time. Even when she's cooking dinner."

Paige shrugged. "I just sort of make little circles in the kitchen or march in place. It's no big deal."

"Well, dear, I did have to explain some things to the church building committee."

She shook her head. "Serves them right for being so nosy."

"You were marching in place on the front porch while filling the bird feeders. That did kind of seem odd to a few of them."

Paige shook her head, then smiled. "Well, look who's here."

Brad made his way over to join the innkeepers with a woman who was likely the reporter following a step behind. "Marissa," he said, smiling down at the dark-haired woman. "Let me introduce you to some very dear friends of mine." He made the introductions and then added, "I'm going to go see if my brother needs anything, but I'll be back."

"You'd better hurry back," Marissa said with a grin.

Though the old LuAnn might have cringed at the familiarity in the reporter's tone, the new and improved LuAnn did not. "I'm so glad to finally meet you. Brad has said some nice things about you."

"I'm glad to hear it, because he has said some nice things about you too. So perhaps we can do a quick interview? Just a couple of quotes for the article I'm doing on First Friday?"

"Sure," LuAnn said. Marissa began asking questions, and the three friends took turns answering them.

When she was done, Marissa put away her notebook and thanked them. "Might I have a word with you, LuAnn?" she asked.

"Of course." She stepped away with Marissa to a quiet corner of the room. "How can I help you?"

The reporter shrugged. "I'm a very direct person, so I'll get right to it. Is there anything going on between you and Brad?"

LuAnn frowned. "We're friends. Why?"

"Well, I'm sure he told you how we met."

"He mentioned he was showing you houses here in Marietta."

"Yes, that's right." Marissa glanced across the room. LuAnn followed her gaze to Brad, who was doing a very poor job of trying not to let them see he was watching. Just to tease him, she waved.

He shook his head and returned the wave.

"See?" Marissa said. "This is exactly why I asked if you two were a thing."

"We're not," LuAnn insisted. "But what do you mean?"

"He talks about you constantly. You look across the room, and you two have a conversation without saying a word." She shook her head. "It doesn't take a reporter to see there's something there."

"You're right about that," LuAnn told her. "I like Brad very much. He was a good Realtor when he was a stranger and we were looking for this inn—although actually we weren't looking for an inn but rather a home for me, but that's a whole other story—and he's a good friend now that I've known him a while."

"But that's all there is to it?" Marissa asked. "Just a friendship?"

Once again LuAnn did a heart check, as her mother used to call it. "Yes," she said with confidence. "That's all there is to it. Just a friendship."

Marissa smiled. "All right," she said. "Thank you for letting me ask."

LuAnn returned the smile. "You're welcome. And thank you for interviewing us about the inn's participation tonight."

That comment turned the conversation in a different direction. After a few minutes, Paige wandered past, and LuAnn intercepted her to make an introduction. Once the reporter and the pastor's wife were deep in conversation, LuAnn excused herself to go and circulate among the guests.

She found Margaret Ashworth, director of the local historical society, cradling her signed photo of an antique camera. "I'm so glad you found something you like," LuAnn said. "Would you like me to put it behind the front desk with your name on it while you mingle with the others?"

Margaret shook her head. "No, I think I'll just hold on to this. My fourth great-grandfather, Rhett Ashworth, was a professor at Marietta College back in the 1860s, and quite involved in the Underground Railroad. There's a story in my family that he, along with a photographer friend from New York, was able to save three escaped slaves using a camera that is reputed to be this very one. The camera itself is in the archives at the college."

"That's amazing!"

"It is. I only wish someone had worked out the details of how that could be. I actually got an email recently from a lovely lady in Canada who told me a similar tale had been handed down in her family. Her ancestors were the slaves that my grandfather helped free—a girl named Mary, her grandfather, and brother. Apparently the brother became quite powerful and well-to-do in Canada, and his charitable foundations still help millions there and abroad to this day. Anyway, she and I have been having a grand time filling in the blanks in our shared stories. I've ordered a smaller print of this picture to send to her as a gift."

"That's wonderful, Margaret. I can't wait to hear how it all turns out."

Brad caught up with LuAnn at the food table. "Quite the First Friday event here, Lu," he said with a grin. "Not only did my brother sell out of his photos, but he also may have found his next true love."

She followed his gaze to where Ellie and Grant were deep in conversation. Though there were plenty of people nearby, those two only had eyes for each other.

"I like Ellie," she told him. "I think she might be a good match for your brother. I got a few good shots of them together."

"Time will tell," he said as he reached for a pear, goat cheese, and walnut lettuce cup.

"She may be calling you soon to help her find a building to rent for her wedding planning business. Unless she's already done that."

"Not yet." He raised his eyebrows. "These little handheld salads are amazing. Did Winnie make them?"

"No." She reached for one. "Winnie is out of town for the weekend, so she made the desserts and bread ahead of time, but we had to make other arrangements for the rest of the food. These came from the food truck parked out back."

"No, it's parked out front," he said. "I saw it when I came in."

"I saw it out back." She nodded toward the loading dock. "Come on. I'll show you."

He shrugged and allowed her to lead him away. "All right."

They wove through the crowd toward the back of the inn where LuAnn triumphantly opened the door to reveal the bright green food truck. "Lettuce Cup You," she said. "Right where I said it would be."

"Fair enough," he said. "But that's not the food truck I saw. Now it's my turn to show you."

She gave him a sideways look as she locked the door. "You realize this is the only food truck that's supposed to be here, right?"

"Come with me and I'll show you that there are at least two here." They linked arms, and Brad led her through the crowd and out the front door. "See, there it is," he said as the door closed behind them.

"Where?"

He led her down to the street and pointed in the direction of the river. "There, see it? It's a black food truck. The lights are off so you can't see the name on it right now, but I saw it very clearly when I arrived. It said, 'I See You Seafood and Sandwiches.'"

"So that truck has been here since what? Five o'clock?" At his nod, she said, "Come on, then. Let's see what they're up to."

"Hold on." Brad grasped LuAnn's elbow to halt her progress. "What are you going to say? You can't tell them they can't park on the street."

She shrugged out of his reach. "It's a food truck. I'll just tell them I want to buy something."

LuAnn marched across the street with Brad trailing behind. The motor of the truck was definitely running, and there appeared to be someone inside the back of it.

She knocked on the window. "Hello?"

Nothing.

"LuAnn," Brad said. "They're obviously not open for business."

"Nonsense. Someone has to be here. Who would leave a truck abandoned with the engine running? I just want to ask why they parked by the inn."

She knocked again and got the same response. "Maybe there's a window on the other side," she said. She walked behind the truck with the intention of seeking another way of getting the owner's attention.

Without warning, the truck lurched forward and zoomed away. "Well, how about that?" LuAnn said. "Someone *was* in there."

"Someone who didn't bother to turn on his headlights," Brad said as the truck screeched around the corner and disappeared.

"That's the second time a food truck has left here in a hurry." She told Brad what happened earlier to Tess.

"I have no explanation," he said as he escorted her back inside. "Unless there's some sort of territorial turf war between food trucks. That's a new one on me, though."

LuAnn hurried back inside to update Janice and Tess on this latest encounter with a food truck.

"You know," Tess said, "I do think the truck that took off this afternoon was dark. Maybe it was the same one."

Brad shook his head. "Two food trucks behaving strangely at the inn. Are you three about to embark on another mystery to solve?"

"We just might be," Janice said as she waved goodbye to Maybelline Rector.

"I don't know, Janice," LuAnn said. "I've had enough sleuthing to last a lifetime."

Tess shook her head. "Oh come on, now. What about our promise to each other?" She stood straighter and put her right hand over her heart. "'We will never be boring or bored, and we will never act our age.'" She dropped her hand. "You have to admit that since we took on ownership of the inn our lives have not been boring."

The remainder of the evening passed in a swirl of shopping, dining, and chatting. When Janice finally turned the key to lock the door after the last guest left, LuAnn let out a long sigh.

"We did it, ladies," she said as she high-fived Tess and then Janice. "Our very first First Friday is in the books. I think it was a success, don't you?"

"I think it was a grand success. Grant's pictures sold out, and we even had a marriage proposal." Tess turned to Janice. "And you and your team did a fabulous job with the food."

"Thank you," Janice said. "But I sure do miss Winnie. I'll be glad when she's back at the stove on Monday morning."

LuAnn reached over to pop a lettuce cup into her mouth and savor the bite. "Me too," she said. "Although I have to admit that Yelp was right about these."

Tess grinned and grabbed two of them. "I agree."

"How about we enjoy these in the kitchen?" Janice suggested.

"As good as that sounds," LuAnn said as she strolled over to the front desk to retrieve the notebook she had hidden there, "I believe I'm just going to head for bed. I am exhausted."

"Hey, kiddo," Tess called. "Great job tonight."

"Thanks," LuAnn said as she climbed the stairs. "Maybe next month I'll turn the planning over to one of you."

They all laughed as she climbed the stairs and practically fell into bed with Huck and Tom curled at her feet. LuAnn's last thought before she fell into the depths of slumber was to give thanks.

And to marvel at the truth of how praise really did keep panic at bay.

CHAPTER SIX

The next morning, in between the café's breakfast and lunch shifts, Ellie and Marsha were seated in the lobby when LuAnn came out of the kitchen, coffee mug in hand. Ellie seemed strangely subdued, and Marsha wore her usual grumpy expression.

"Good morning," LuAnn said as she passed by them on her way to the inn's office behind the front desk.

Neither responded.

LuAnn found Tess seated at the desk, her head buried in what appeared to be a pile of receipts. She looked up as LuAnn paused in the doorway.

"What's up with those two?" LuAnn asked. "Even at her worst, Marsha hasn't ignored a greeting. And Ellie is downright glum. I thought after the way she and Grant hit it off last night she would be practically giddy this morning."

"Who knows?" Tess said. "Maybe they're tired. They're only just now having some breakfast. But remember, I've already said there's something off with those two."

The bell chimed, alerting the women that someone had opened the inn's front door. LuAnn turned to the office doorway to see Grant walking toward the cousins' table.

"Good morning, ladies," he said to Ellie and Marsha. Then he turned to spy LuAnn. "And good morning to you too. Have you had a chance to look at your photos from last night?"

"Not yet," said LuAnn. "We've been busy this morning."

"No problem. I can wait. Brad told me you got some of Ellie and me, and I was just wondering how they turned out."

LuAnn smiled at him. "Tell you what. I'm not going to do anything with them until after the wedding, but the minute I do, I'll send you what I got."

Grant nodded. "That sounds fine."

"Oh, Grant," Ellie said, her downcast demeanor now banished, "thank you so much for taking time for us today. Isn't it wonderful of him, Marsha?"

Marsha made no attempt to respond. Rather, she took another bite of her croissant and stared out the window toward the river.

"You'll have to excuse her," Ellie said. "She's a little out of sorts. Apparently she took her sleeping pill instead of her sinus pill when we returned from our outing yesterday afternoon. She went right to sleep and only just woke up less than an hour ago."

This time Marsha's response was swift. Her gaze swung to stare at Ellie. Even from her spot behind the front desk, LuAnn could see the rage on her face.

For a split second Ellie's eyes widened. Then she quickly recovered to focus her attention on Grant again. "Won't you join us and have a cup of coffee? Marsha says the croissants are divine. I'll have to trust her word on the matter, because I'm limiting myself to fruit and a little yogurt this morning."

"Thank you, no. I don't mind sitting with you until you're finished, though."

Marsha pushed her plate away and stood. "I'm done." She looked down at Ellie. "I'll go and get our purses. Don't think of leaving without me."

A slow smile fluttered onto Ellie's face. "Why on earth would we leave without you? You're such fun."

LuAnn cringed and glanced back at Tess. "Are you hearing this?" she whispered.

Tess nodded and gave her an I-told-you-so look. When LuAnn returned her attention to the pair in the café, they were heading her way.

"Before we go," Grant said, "I just want to thank you again for last night. I never expected to completely sell out of all of my photographs."

Ellie rested a protective hand on his arm. "They sold because they're amazing," she said, looking up adoringly at Grant.

The normally boisterous Grimes brother seemed at a loss for words. A deep flush climbed into his cheeks.

"They are amazing," Tess affirmed. "In fact, we've received an email this morning requesting prints of several of them. I guess someone must have decided after they left that they had to have them." She shrugged. "Want me to forward the email?"

"Yes, please," he said. "Although I don't know when I can get around to making more prints. I do have a client here who needs not only a business, but a place to live."

"Don't be silly," Ellie said. "I don't mind if we stop by your office so you can print out whatever copies the buyer wants. How long could that possibly take?"

He shook his head. "I don't do digital, Ellie. My photographs are taken using an old-school film camera. I have my own darkroom and develop my own prints."

"Oh."

LuAnn watched her expression change. Did she seem disappointed?

"There's Marsha," Grant said as he nodded toward the stairs. "It looks like the three of us are off for a day of house hunting."

"About that," Ellie said. "I'm wondering if you might be able to show me some rental properties too. I've been thinking about things, and now I'm not so certain I actually want to live above the store, so to speak. Maybe a building for the planning business and a little cottage somewhere for me to go home to at night?"

"I may have just the place," he said. "Last night Justin O'Hara mentioned that he's ready to lease the house he flipped over on Cherry Street. The house is very small, though, with just one bedroom and one bath. It does have a nice yard and is newly redone inside and out."

"It sounds perfect. Is Cherry Street anywhere near the river?"

"It is. Would you like me to make the call and arrange a time to look at it?"

"Oh, Grant, yes please."

Marsha bypassed them to go and stand by the front door holding two purses and looking as if she'd been hired by the CIA to keep everyone in the inn safe. LuAnn suppressed a grin as Grant tried not to stare.

"Are we leaving, or have we decided to stay a while longer?" Marsha called from the door.

"Why don't I get you both in the car and then I'll make the call?" Grant smiled at LuAnn and Tess. "Have a great day, ladies."

"You too," Tess said, and LuAnn nodded.

Grant's eyes widened, and he grinned. Ellie allowed him to lead her outside with Marsha marching a step behind.

"Poor guy," LuAnn mused as the door closed behind the unlikely trio.

"Oh, I don't know," Tess said. "He seems smitten with Ellie, so I doubt it will bother him to share her with her grouchy cousin for a little while."

LuAnn agreed. "And if she's looking at a one-bedroom, my guess is that Cousin Marsha isn't sticking around indefinitely."

When Grant dropped the two women off later that afternoon, they were so deep in conversation that they must not have noticed the open office door and that LuAnn was seated out of sight at the desk. The café had closed, and all the laundry and cleaning had been done for the day, so the inn was so quiet that LuAnn could hear the clock ticking.

"You can't possibly be serious about settling down here," she heard Marsha say.

LuAnn set her work aside and leaned forward slowly so as to not make a noise that might alert them to her presence.

Instantly convicted, she leaned back and allowed the antique chair to squeak. Then she cleared her throat. Surely they'd heard her.

"Why not?" Ellie's laughter held no humor as their footsteps rattled across the floor and up the steps. "It's a perfectly good house, and I love it. And Grant Grimes is absolutely charming."

"You're being ridiculous. You know we won't be—"

Their voices faded away, ending any ability for LuAnn to listen in further. The inn's phone rang, and she reached to answer it.

"I'm sorry to bother you on a Saturday," Beverly said. "But Thorn said it was all right that I call because you ladies don't take the weekend off."

"That is true," she said. "It's a hazard of being innkeepers, but we love what we do, so it's fine. Congratulations on your engagement, by the way."

"Thank you." The happiness in Bev's voice was impossible to miss. LuAnn's smile rose before the soon-to-be Mrs. Thornton spoke again. "I never expected the Lord would put us back together, but He sure has."

"Yes, He has," LuAnn agreed. "So what can I do for you?"

"Laura is determined to get started on the wedding planning, but I'm not sure how to get in touch with that sweet lady who volunteered to do it for us. I believe her name is Ellie. Would you be able to help with that?"

"I would indeed. Let me transfer you to her room."

"Thank you. I appreciate it."

LuAnn pushed the button to transfer the call, but instead of the ring she expected to hear, she got a busy signal. She pushed the button to talk to Beverly again.

"Bev, Ellie must be on the phone. I can go up and tell her you're trying to get ahold of her. I'll give her your number."

"I don't want to be a bother."

"Nonsense. I'll just go and tell her the bride would like to speak to her."

Beverley giggled. "I guess I'm going to have to get used to that," she said. "And I do thank you for going to all of this trouble for me."

LuAnn hung up, jotted Bev's phone number on a sticky note, and went upstairs to Ellie's room. The argument must have ended because she heard nothing but silence when she reached the third floor.

A knock at Ellie's door produced more silence. Then the door opened just enough for Ellie to stick her head out. "Yes?"

LuAnn held the note out to her. "Beverly Thornton called for you. The woman who got engaged last night. She wants to talk to you about getting started on the wedding planning."

"That's wonderful." Ellie gave her a brilliant smile and completely ignored the note. "Would you mind getting as much information as you can from her so I can begin planning?"

LuAnn shook her head. "What do you mean?"

"Oh, you know. Find out what colors she wants to use, what flowers she likes, where she wants to hold the ceremony and the reception. Just the general information."

"General information. Right," LuAnn echoed as she shrugged. "I suppose I could do that."

Ellie put on a grateful expression. "Thank you, LuAnn. Marsha has taken a migraine pill and gone to bed. I'm afraid our house shopping has done her in. Migraines are just awful, you know."

"I don't know," LuAnn admitted, "but I can imagine they are."

"The worst. And when she gets this way I seem to be the only one who can help her."

"It must have come on suddenly," LuAnn said. "I couldn't help hearing you two when you arrived, and she sounded fine."

"Migraines are like that. One minute you're fine, and the next you're down for the count." She shrugged. "Well, thank you for handling the new bride consultation for me."

And then the door shut, leaving LuAnn staring at the closed door in stunned silence. "All right, then," she muttered under her breath. "I will do just that."

After all, she was a planner. She'd hosted more events than she could count, including a very successful First Friday. How difficult could it be to ask a few questions so a wedding planner would know what the bride prefers?

"Piece of cake." She grinned to herself. "Wedding cake, of course."

She walked back down to the office, passing Robin on the staircase carrying a load of towels up to the storage closet. "Everything okay?" she asked LuAnn.

"Probably," LuAnn said. "But you might want to be extra quiet around Marsha's room. Ellie said Marsha has a migraine."

"No problem," Robin said. "The vacuuming is done. I need to replace towels in a few of the rooms, but I can wait to take them theirs later."

"Yes, that's probably best." LuAnn hurried back to the phone and dialed Beverly's number. "Hi, Bev," she said when her friend answered.

"Hello," Bev said cheerily.

"Ellie has asked me to stand in for her and ask a few questions about your wedding preferences. Can you do that now?"

"Ready as I will ever be, but you have to understand I am hardly a blushing bride. In fact, the last thing that has been on my mind for a very long time is wedding preferences. Retirement plans and wrinkle cream, yes. Wedding cake and bridesmaid dresses, no."

LuAnn chuckled. "I completely understand. So maybe the two of us can figure this out together."

May 4, 1860

Three days passed with no word from Jason. Prudence was pressing her best dress for Sunday services when he appeared on the porch with an exhausted smile and a request for a plate of beans and cornbread and a soft chair to rest his weary bones. She put away the iron, hung the dress back on its peg in the bedroom, then hurried to fuss over him, treating him like a hero returned. And though Jason protested that he was not in need of such treatment, she offered it all the same.

Finally, with his belly full and his leg propped up with pillows, he closed his eyes. She tiptoed past, careful not to waken him, but he lifted his hand to catch her.

His tired eyes opened, and a smile rose. "Wife, thee is such a blessing to me."

She leaned down to press a kiss to his forehead. "Rest," she told him, "and later be prepared to tell me all about thy adventures these three days."

His nod was slow but sleep swift. Prudence lingered until she heard his familiar snore, and then went to see to little Moses. His whimper threatened to become a cry that would wake his papa, so she carried him outside to play in the sunshine.

Patience joined them but remained quiet while the little boy ran in circles around her. When Moses grew bored of his games, Prudence scooped him up and walked down toward the river for her daily check of the secret spot where messages were left and plans were made.

For several weeks, there had been no indication of any need for her to assist with the Underground Railroad's efforts here. Either the crossings had become more dangerous with the rumors of war, or slaves were being removed upriver rather than here in Marietta.

As she always did, Prudence held her breath as she rounded the corner. The breath went out of her when she saw the sign. Two packages. Tonight.

She gasped for air as she settled her little one more firmly on her hip. The respite from danger had ended. Tonight she would once again risk her life for the lives of others.

It was a fair trade given what the Lord had done for her on the cross, this she knew to be true. But each time she made the crossing it was more difficult than the last. It seemed that as Moses grew, so did her fear that some night she would not survive to come home to him.

Prudence snatched up the ribbon and tucked it into her apron pocket. With the dappled sunshine filtering through the trees and a fresh breeze dancing past, there would be time enough to think on such things. For now, she would enjoy her son. Soon enough, she would sit at her husband's feet and hear his tale.

And soon enough, she would step out into the black of night with a prayer that the Lord would not only follow her out on her way but that He would also bless the work of their hands on that night and bring each of them safely home to their beds.

CHAPTER SEVEN

"B efore Marla's wedding a few months ago, I had forgotten how much went into wedding planning," Janice said as she leaned against the open door of LuAnn's sitting room with the cat making figure eights around her ankles.

An array of flyers and catalogs littered LuAnn's desk, and an already lengthy list of notes for Ellie seemed to be growing by the minute. LuAnn added one more action item to the page and set her pen aside to pet Huck, who had claimed the place of honor in her lap.

"When I agreed to do a little legwork for Ellie while she house hunted—and frankly I think also while she and Grant enjoyed a lunch date or two—I didn't realize I would be doing all this." She leaned back in her chair and grinned. "But you know what? I'm enjoying it immensely. These young brides are so clever with all their ideas. I could spend hours online just going from site to site looking at the beautiful weddings."

Janice chuckled. "It all just makes me tired. When Lawrence and I got married, we had our ceremony at the church and the reception in the hall next door. I wore a dress my mother sewed for me, and we made the veil out of yards of tulle and a head-band we covered in satin. There was punch and cake and my friends, and the table was decorated with the bouquets from my bridesmaids."

"I remember," LuAnn said with a smile. "It was a beautiful wedding, and you were a beautiful bride."

Her friend's face softened for a moment, and she appeared to be lost in thought. Then, just like that, the moment was gone.

"Yes, well, I thought you might like to know that that reporter—Marissa?—from the local paper called. The article about First Friday was so well received, she would like to do an interview with us for a longer feature."

"That's wonderful. We've already gotten several calls from guests who heard about us from the paper. Imagine what a feature interview will accomplish."

Janice shrugged and leaned down to scratch Tom between the ears. "Well, we can only accommodate so many guests here each night, so there's not much use in doing too much advertising. Unless we want to add on to the property," she said.

"Goodness, no," LuAnn declared. "Can you imagine what that would be like? Some days it seems like yesterday we were seeing to the renovations of the inn. Other days I try to remember what that was like, and I simply can't."

"It was hot, tiring, and a lot of trouble," Janice said. "But goodness gracious goat, I wouldn't have missed any of it for the world. And I am very glad we did this. Can you imagine what your life would be like if we hadn't decided to go for this adventure?"

"Oh no," LuAnn mused. "I would probably be sitting in my living room, drinking a cup of tea and wishing for something to do. I was so lost after I retired."

"Well, what was once lost is now found," Janice said. "The other reason I came up here is because Winnie and I are going to make a quick run to the grocery store for some things to go in a new soup she's experimenting with. Some kind of Moroccan chicken soup, I think she said. Anyway, we wondered if you would like to come along. We'll be back in plenty of time to prep for the lunch crowd. Winnie is going with a simple menu—I think she's still recovering from last week's cooking ahead for Friday night's bash."

"I do love soups, but I've got one more call to make to the florist. Can I join you this afternoon when you start making this masterpiece?"

"You sure can," Janice said. "In the meantime, have fun, Madame Wedding Planner."

"I'm having a great time, but that would be Madame Temporary Wedding Planner, if you please," LuAnn said as she watched Janice disappear out of view.

But was she temporary? The more LuAnn thought about it, the more she realized that she was the wedding planner now, and Ellie was merely the one who was barking instructions as she breezed out the door in some fabulous outfit with Grant driving the getaway car.

"How long does it take to find a house and a business, for goodness' sake?"

"I don't know about other people," Tess said as she passed by LuAnn's door with a mug in her hand. "But it took the three of us about five minutes. And here we are."

"Yes, here we are," LuAnn echoed as she set a reluctant Huck on his feet and rose to stand in the doorway. "Where are you going?"

"Downstairs to adjust Ellie's and Marsha's bills. "Apparently they both dropped their room phones sometime this weekend. The phones are in pieces. And the lines in Marsha's room are pulled out of the wall. Not disconnected, mind you. Torn out, as in broken wiring. She wasn't in her room when I was up there just now, but Ellie showed me and said Marsha must have tugged too hard when she carried the phone into the bathroom or something. I've called the phone company to come re-wire the room."

LuAnn's jaw dropped. "I don't even know where to start. What in the world were they doing?"

"Who knows? This is Ellie and Marsha we're talking about. If we want to keep the inn in one piece we may want to think about shutting down temporarily and help them look for that new house." Tess headed down the stairs.

After clearing her desk, LuAnn headed down to the office where Tess was finishing up a phone call.

"Good news," Tess said. "That was Justin O'Hara. Apparently Ellie would like to lease his fully furnished rental over on Cherry Street and told him that we could vouch for her as a good tenant."

They shared a laugh, and then LuAnn sobered. "What did you say?"

"That we would be thrilled to recommend that she rent his place," she said. "Because it gets her out of here. That last part I didn't mention. But I did ask if he had good insurance on the house."

"Did he wonder why you asked?"

Tess shook her head. "He did not but said that he would check and make sure he was covered for any rental damages."

"As long as he's insured, he should be fine."

"He did say if we vouched for her, she could pick up her keys as soon as the lease is signed."

"Well, hallelujah to that. Have you told Grant you were called as a reference?"

"Not yet. Between the telephones and the receipts from Friday that I've been going through, I haven't had a chance."

"Want me to?"

Tess gave her a grateful look. "Would you mind?"

"Not at all." LuAnn glanced out the front door and frowned. "Is that the food truck again?"

"The one with the lettuce cups? They were amazing, by the way. Although I have to wonder why they don't just call them handheld salads or something else that explains how delicious they are. To me, a lettuce cup is absolutely not an adequate description."

"I don't know why they're called that either," LuAnn said. "But focus. It isn't the same food truck. There was another one out front that night. A black truck with some kind of seafood restaurant logo on the side. Brad spied it when he came early for the event on Friday and asked me about it. I told him our truck was out back, so he showed me there was another in the front. It took off while we were standing behind it trying to investigate."

"That's very odd."

"It was," LuAnn said as she moved toward the door.

Tess rose to follow her. "Is it the same one?"

"Well," LuAnn said as she dodged a pair of guests who were headed for the café, "it is black, but the logo on the side is different."

"Charlie's Mexi-ribbean Grilled Cheese," Tess said. "Interesting name. I wonder what Mexican and Caribbean food tastes like on a grilled cheese?"

"Couldn't be any odder than walking around with a salad in your hand," LuAnn said.

"Hey, those lettuce cups were really good," Tess protested. "I especially liked the chicken with peanut sauce."

"They were delicious," LuAnn agreed. "Winnie and I have already been experimenting with recipes to make our own versions for next First Friday. Maybe we'll try a Mexi-ribbean grilled cheese version."

"You can experiment on me anytime, my friend," Tess said. "I'll be your happy guinea pig, although I don't know about the... hey..." She nodded toward the food truck now pulling away from the curb across the street. "Looks like the grilled cheeses are hitting the road."

"I guess we will never know what a Mexi-ribbean grilled cheese tastes like unless we make our own," LuAnn said with a shrug. "Oh, look, here comes Paige. I cannot believe she hasn't had that baby yet."

Paige stepped inside the inn with a smile on her face.

"I wish I had looked like her when I was pregnant," Tess said. "She's absolutely radiant. I, however, was a basketball with toothpick legs and swollen ankles."

"Sounds lovely," LuAnn quipped as she hurried over to greet the expectant mother. "Come and sit down," she said. "How about a cup of tea? I have decaf."

"I'm fine, thank you," Paige said. "But I will take you up on your offer to sit down. I've been walking for the better part of an hour in hopes I might convince this child that today would be an excellent day for a birthday celebration."

"But?"

"But he or she is not listening."

LuAnn laughed. "Get used to that. I taught school for thirty-five years, so I know a thing or two about kids who don't cooperate."

"Speaking of not cooperating," Paige said gently, "I'm here on a mission from my husband. He's been trying to reach the wedding planner for the Thornton wedding, and she's not returning his calls."

"I see." *Praise before panic.* LuAnn smiled. "Well then, I suppose I might be able to answer any questions he might have. I've been helping Ellie."

"Oh, good. I can't speak for what his questions are, but if you would just give him a call when you get a chance, that would be great."

"Of course." LuAnn looked up and spied the telephone company truck pull up out front and a man get out. "No problem. I'll get right on that."

And the caterer. And the florist.

But first, the telephone guy.

"So how do you like the Bible study?" Paige asked as she climbed to her feet with great difficulty.

"I can't think of a more timely topic than that one," LuAnn told her. "'Praise before panic' has become my go-to phrase."

Paige glanced over toward the technician, now stepping inside the door with his clipboard. "Yes, I can see why. Now, I'll get out of your way so you can handle whatever he's here for."

LuAnn gave her friend a hug. "He can wait. How about I help you to your car?"

"Not a chance," she said. "My doctor told me if I want this baby to hurry up and get here, I need to walk more. I'm parked down the block, but I may go around the opposite direction to get more steps in."

"Well, good luck. I'll see you at Bible study tomorrow night."

"Unless I'm busy having this baby," Paige said, her fingers crossed.

"Well then, in that case I'll see the two of you later in the week," LuAnn told her, and then waved as the door closed behind her. "Now, the telephone." The technician walked past her toward the front desk. "Tess, the telephone man is here."

While Tess took care of showing the man where the damage had occurred, LuAnn dialed the real estate office. Saffron picked up with a cheery, "Grimes Realty."

"Hello, Saffron, it's LuAnn. Is your dad around?"

"No, but Uncle Brad is here. Will he do?"

LuAnn smiled to herself. "He'll do just fine, thanks."

"Okay, but before I transfer you, I have to tell you that the First Friday bash at your place was awesome. I hope you're planning on doing more of them."

"We haven't had a chance to discuss it yet, but I think we will."

"I'll have to let Justin know. I had no idea he was a patron of the arts, but apparently he bought a bunch of my dad's photos."

"Imagine that," LuAnn said with a grin. She was still grinning when Saffron said goodbye and transferred her to Brad's line.

"Great to hear from you, LuAnn," he said. "What's up?"

She related the news about the phone call from Justin. "We thought Grant would want to know we gave Ellie a glowing reference."

Brad chuckled. "That's great, but I think my little brother has been enjoying taking Ellie house hunting."

"From what I understand, she's also looking for a place to locate her wedding planning business, so Grant may yet find more excuses to be with her."

"That is true." Brad paused. "Speaking of the wedding, is it true that you're planning to make some of those salad cups for the reception?"

"Umm..." She shook her head, though she knew full well he couldn't see her reaction. "Why would you ask that? I don't think Ellie has finalized the food yet."

"Oh." He actually sounded disappointed. "Grant told me, I think. Or maybe it was Ellie. I did see her this morning. Then I saw Winnie and Janice at the grocery store. They were experimenting with some soup that sounds amazing. Janice asked if I wanted to come and help with the taste testing this afternoon, but I had to decline. I'm showing Marissa houses after lunch."

"And all of this added up to me making lettuce cups for the reception?"

"I do remember Ellie specifically mentioning it." He paused. "But maybe she just misunderstood. Anyway, I'll pass on the good news to my brother."

There was a pause on the other end of the line. "LuAnn, can I ask you a question?"

"Of course," she said. "What's up?"

"Okay, so I know my brother has been kind of interested in Ellie. I don't think it's just related to finding her a place to live and a work space."

"That's not a question."

"No, it isn't," he said. "But this is. Do you get the impression she's serious about him?"

"Well," she said as she considered the question, "I was there when they first met, and there was definitely something there. And I've seen her looking very happy when she leaves to meet him. I've seen him looking very happy when he comes in before or after their house-hunting trips. So yes, I'm going to guess there's something going on between them."

"I know Grant is nuts about her. She's even got him wearing something other than those stupid Hawaiian shirts, and that in itself is a miracle. But do you think *she* is serious about *him*?"

LuAnn thought a moment. "You know, I really don't know."

"Me neither. I just hope he doesn't get hurt."

They hung up with LuAnn still shaking her head. Was she not doing enough for this wedding? Now she would be cooking the food too?

She tucked her phone into her pocket and stalked upstairs. Enough was enough.

"Hey, Tess?" she called from the second-floor landing.

Her friend stuck her head out of Ellie's room. "Yes?"

"Unless you need me for something, I'm going to go up to my desk to work on wedding details until Winnie and Janice get back. Would you mind letting me know when Ellie returns?"

"Not at all," Tess said.

LuAnn made her way back upstairs to tumble down the rabbit trail that was planning the Thornton wedding.

CHAPTER EIGHT

May 4, 1860

Prudence returned to the farmhouse to find Jason sitting on the porch steps waiting for her. When Moses spied him, he wriggled out of her arms to hurry off in his direction. Prudence tucked her fingers into her apron pockets, feeling the ribbon along with the dread of telling Jason about tonight.

So she said nothing but settled alongside him on the porch to offer a kiss on his cheek. Moses was not content with a mere kiss. He wanted his papa to run and play.

Though Jason made the attempt, he soon returned to the porch. At that, Moses wailed in protest. At the sound of the child crying, Patience came hurrying around the corner.

Soon the honks of the goose mixed with the cries of the little boy. "Enough," Jason said as he gently clapped his hands. "Quiet, please."

Moses looked up at his father, eyes wide. Patience merely skittered away to watch from the far end of the porch.

"Come and sit with me," Jason told Moses. "I've brought you something."

Of course the little boy didn't understand his father's words, but he was intrigued by what he held in his hand. Moses came close, eventually climbing into Jason's lap.

Jason opened his palm and showed Moses a rock crusted in a dark color and striped through the center with colors of blue, green, and gray. Moses snatched the rock and threw it, and Patience hurried to bring it back.

When the goose deposited the rock at Jason's feet, he retrieved it and handed it back to Moses. The game continued until the child tired of it and wandered over to play with blocks of wood in the sunshine.

"I believe I am owed a story," Prudence said as she kept a watchful eye on her son. "Will thee oblige?"

Jason gave her a sideways look. "I will," he said. "But first I owe thee an apology. Thy argument against me going was correct. I ought not to have tried it."

"I made no argument, Husband," she protested.

"Perhaps," he said gently, "but thy silence spoke quite loudly."

She managed a quick smile. "Perhaps I did have some reservations. But I did take care not to speak of them."

Jason reached over to take Prudence's hand in his. "As befitting a good wife." He paused. "I nearly turned back before I reached Marietta. The injury that makes me a poor excuse for a farmer also made me unfit for the long walk to New Concord."

"New Concord?" Prudence gasped. "But that is some fifty miles north, is it not?"

"It is, but as we who had pledged to travel with the men from the college gathered on the steps there, I was fortunate to strike up a conversation with a fellow I assumed to be a farmer like me."

Moses giggled, and they both turned to see the cause. Patience had waddled over to where the boy was playing and was nudging one of the blocks with her beak.

"I warrant that bird is not like any other I have seen," Jason said. "But back to the story. This fellow, he took note of me but in a most kindly way. Next I knew I had been chosen out of the crowd to be among those who were assigned to watch over the instruments that would be used for measuring the rocks they expected to find."

"Was that a fortunate assignment?"

He smiled, and her heart warmed. "Fortunate indeed, for these instruments were heavy and required not only guarding but also transporting by wagon."

"So there was no walking?" she asked as her smile broadened.

"There was walking," he said as he rubbed his leg, "though not as much as there could have been."

"Praise the Lord for this."

"And for an always faithful wife who remembers her husband in her frequent prayers," Jason added.

Prudence leaned into his embrace. "Tell me everything," she said. "What did the men from the college find? Were they certain there was no threat of war to be blamed for this? And why New Concord? I certainly thought the location would be much closer. It looked nearly overhead when we saw it."

"So many questions," Jason said with a laugh. "Have a care to allow answers, Wife."

Prudence grinned, and pressed her index finger to her lips to show him she would remain silent while he spoke. Much as she wished to continue with her questions, she would not.

"The men from the college had a guess as to what had happened before they set out to hunt for the rocks. Some of the men specialize in the study of meteorites, and so they knew what to look for. As word spread that the men from the college were coming, people came out to tell their stories. Many saw the rocks fall, and some say they looked like blackbirds flying toward the ground. Others only heard the event or felt the ground rumble."

"As we did," Prudence offered.

"Indeed." Jason shifted positions and looked past her to where Moses was still playing with his blocks. "I might still be out with the men except for the discovery of a rock twice the size of our boy there. It took five of us to load it into the wagon. It was rushed back to the college for examination, and I went along with it."

"And how did thee come to be chosen for this?"

Jason ducked his head and gave her a sideways look. "I volunteered."

"I see."

"It was a curious event. Does thee not admit curiosity?"

"I do. Imagine a rock of that size falling from the sky? I cannot, and yet it did. Why do these things happen?"

Jason nodded. "The meteorite fell to earth for reasons the professor tried to explain. There are men whose lives are dedicated to the study of such things."

Moses let out a squeal and tossed a block into the air.

"Perhaps someday thy son will be one of those men. Can thee see it? Our Moses studying at the college?" Prudence shook her head. "I truly cannot, and yet he very well might."

"He might," Jason said. "I want much more for him than I have to offer here."

Prudence wrapped her arm around his and leaned her head on his shoulder. "Wishing for more for thy child is well and good enough, but thy wife is perfectly content. Wish for nothing more than a long life, and I shall be happy."

Jason patted her arm. "I could want nothing more than a long life with thee." He paused. "Does thee forgive me?"

"Has thee told me all thy stories of this adventure yet?"

"Not yet," he said.

"Then proceed, and perhaps I shall find forgiveness in my heart." She playfully nudged him with her elbow. "Though I make no promises. I am a woman deeply wounded."

Jason laughed with her, then shook his head. "I cannot begin to do the description justice. There were rocks of a similar kind found a great distance apart, more than seven or eight miles at last count. It was as if the Lord Himself had thrown a boulder the size of a house toward earth, and it shattered into pieces before landing. What was brought back to Marietta College was the largest, but there were so many more."

"Were they just waiting on the ground to be found?" she asked as Patience scurried off to chase something in the grass.

"Some were. Others were found half-buried in fields where farmers had only just been plowing. At least one has ruined a good strong fence at the edge of a pasture, and another took aim at a homestead but only just dented a door." He paused as if recalling the sight. "It took a team of men the better half of an afternoon to free the rock that was returned to Marietta." He grimaced. "I am not proud of the fact that I also volunteered for that duty."

"With thy injuries such as they are?" she demanded, eyes wide.

"Enough of that," he said with a wink. "I am but a man, Prudence, and a man sometimes attempts things he wishes he could still complete. The fact that I am still able to walk adequately and have arrived on thy doorstep to tell the tale should be sufficient for thee."

Prudence gave Jason a look that let him know exactly what she thought of that statement. His injuries had never bothered her, though it plagued her that she could do very little to relieve the pain he suffered from them.

"Husband, thee is home again. That alone is sufficient," she said. "All else is blessing for which I give thanks."

"As do I."

Moses toddled over to tug on Prudence's sleeve. "I believe thy son is hungry again. Once I've fed him his meal, I will begin preparing ours. Shall I bring out the newspapers for thee to read?"

He smiled. "I've been to the place where all of the news seems to be written lately. Perhaps it is time for me to read more in my Bible. Might I trouble thee to bring it to me?"

She snatched up Moses, then leaned down to give Jason a kiss on his forehead. A moment later, she brought back his Bible and handed it to him.

"Oh, I almost forgot," Jason told her. "I met a man in New Concord who'd come to take photographs of the meteorites. His employer sent him out to take photographs of whatever he found interesting. He happened to see the meteorite himself and followed it to where he joined up with us. He has indicated he wishes to come and photograph our boulder at Marietta College. Should he decide to do this, I have offered him hospitality at our home."

Prudence suppressed a frown, happy that Jason was now looking down at his Bible instead of back at her. "Though I am certain this man is nice enough, are thee certain he is a trustworthy friend?"

Jason looked up and swiveled to face her. "I am sure he is a good man, and it was an offer made in passing. Likely he received many such offers, and from men whose hospitality would be much more grand than ours."

She attempted a smile. "Yes, perhaps." But as she walked away, her heart held concern where peace should have dwelt.

CHAPTER NINE

E llie, we really have to stay on topic."

Ellie's room was still being cleaned, so LuAnn had elected to speak to the frustrating woman in her own apartment rather than in the more public areas of the inn. Now she was wishing she hadn't allowed Ellie access to her private space. She was even more frustrated because having to consult with Ellie meant she missed out on Winnie's Moroccan soup.

Rather than remaining on the settee in the shared sitting area where LuAnn had situated her, Ellie was now drifting around the room exclaiming over every painting, pillow, and potted plant.

Huck had given up following her and opted for a spot on LuAnn's lap. Tom climbed onto the back of the chair and eyed the stranger with a wary glare.

"I know, but I am just amazed that you've had such good fortune with these orchids," Ellie said as she picked up one of Janice's prize cymbidiums off the shelf in front of the window. "My mother grew them, but I'm just hopeless. Forget the green thumb for me. I wasn't born with the gardening gene!"

She returned the plant to the shelf, but in the wrong place and far too close to the edge. LuAnn took a deep breath and resisted the urge to move the orchid to its correct spot.

"Yes, well, gardening isn't for everyone. Now, speaking of flowers, what did you decide as far as the arrangements on the...Ellie?"

Ellie was staring out the window and seemed deep in thought. LuAnn shook her head.

"Ellie?"

No reaction. Tom stretched out his claws and yawned.

"Ellie? Is there something out there that is more important than the Thornton wedding?" It was a rude question, but LuAnn had quite reached the end of her patience with the woman.

"Yes, sorry." Ellie turned back toward LuAnn with a penitent expression. "I just love the view from up here. It's absolutely gorgeous."

"It is. I often get lost in thought when I ought to be paying attention at my desk. The view is even prettier there."

"But I don't see a desk. May I look?"

"Only if, after I allow you to have a look, you promise to sit down over there on the settee and not get up until we're done finalizing the details for the Thorntons. Thorn is a good friend to all of us here at the inn, and he's waited a long time to have his happily ever after. We need to do everything we can to make his day perfect."

"I promise," Ellie said.

"All right." LuAnn gently placed Huck on the floor and led Ellie into her own sitting room. She pulled open the drapes to show off the beautiful view.

Ellie gasped. "Oh, it's absolutely breathtaking. I can't imagine anything lovelier." She walked around the room, then wandered into LuAnn's bedroom. Her gaze drifted down to the photograph on LuAnn's nightstand. "Don't you just adore this man's work? He is so talented." She picked up the photograph and held it to her chest. "I own this one too."

LuAnn was more than a little irritated that this woman was in her bedroom. "Yes, I remember. You were the first person to purchase anything from Grant. I wasn't surprised when this one sold first. Of all his photographs, this is my favorite."

"Yes," she said, continuing to hold the photo against her. "He's brilliant. And so handsome too."

"Yes, all right," LuAnn said. "Now you've seen the view. Why don't we go back and finish our planning?"

But Ellie remained in place, her stance like that of an obstinate toddler refusing to give up her favorite toy or be called inside for dinner. Huck lifted his head as if watching the show.

"Ellie," LuAnn said in the tone she took with her more frustrating students. "Put the photograph down. We have work to do."

"Yes, of course." She did as she was told, though she cast what appeared to be one last longing look at the view before LuAnn snapped the curtains shut.

"Come on, Huck," LuAnn said. The dog scooted out, and she closed the door behind them. They walked back to the common area and resumed their seats.

"You're really lucky, LuAnn," Ellie said dreamily. "You live in this beautiful inn, and you have these great friends, and you're drop-dead gorgeous. Everyone loves you. Grant's brother said so himself. You just really have a great life. Even your pets are cute."

LuAnn sat back, astonished, as Tom claimed her lap and Huck jumped onto the chair across from them. "I don't know what to say."

Ellie shrugged. "You don't have to say anything. It just is what it is." She nodded toward the meeting notes that LuAnn had provided. "You're also very well organized. If you ever need a new job, I would hire you in a heartbeat."

"Well, thank you. But perhaps we ought to get back to the reason we're here. Take a look at my ideas for each category and see what you think. I've provided several choices, so basically we just need to narrow everything down to one of each."

"Yes." Ellie reached for the list, then grabbed a pen from the table beside her. "Let's see what we've got here." In what seemed like seconds, she perused each section and made her selection. "Great job. I like it. Here you go."

LuAnn accepted the list from Ellie and looked down to see what she had chosen. "Okay, so you like the rose gold and pink theme. Good. I do too."

"That simplifies things, don't you think? I like a clean white palette and then a pop of color here and there using the theme shades. It's kind of my signature thing for brides this year."

"But you've chosen red roses." LuAnn looked up at her. "Was that intentional?"

Ellie snatched the list back. "Oh my goodness, no." She thrust the page back at LuAnn. "Everything white except pops of color. Focus, LuAnn."

LuAnn bit her tongue. She needed to praise before panic, and fast.

Likely sensing the change in mood, Tom stretched, then jumped to the floor where he disappeared under the coffee table. Huck quickly left his perch on the other chair and claimed LuAnn's lap for himself.

LuAnn let out a long breath. If Ellie hadn't decided to call this impromptu meeting, she might have had Laura and Bev as backup. "All right. And our pops of color will be where?"

"I trust you to decide," Ellie said. "Now let's talk about money. Have you already gone over these choices with Beverly? She'll need to approve the funds before we spend them." She paused to let out a dramatic sigh. "I'm sorry I've been so busy with finding a house and business space."

"Congratulations, by the way," LuAnn said as she scratched the dog's furry head.

Ellie lifted a carefully plucked brow. "Excuse me?"

"On the lease. Justin called us for references, and when we vouched for you he said you would be getting a lease soon. He just needs someone to come pick up the paperwork."

"I'll have Grant do that. He's such a dear."

"Sure, okay. Anyway, back to payments. The amounts are listed beside each entry. For all but the caterer we need to pay half up front and the rest day of. The caterer needs three-fourths due to costs for ordering ingredients and hiring staff."

"That sounds reasonable. If you'll just ask the happy couple to approve the expenses, we can finalize the arrangements, and the vendors can invoice them." She stood. "Now, if we are done...?"

"We are."

Ellie flounced her way to the door. "Thank you for all your help, LuAnn. You really are a good person. Grant was right about you."

LuAnn waited until Ellie was gone to walk over and open the door to her bedroom. She went over to open the drapes, and Tom leaped onto the bed, making circles in his favorite spot until it was exactly right for curling up. LuAnn leaned against the windowsill and looked out over the treetops to the river. This *was* a beautiful view. And she *did* have a good life.

The next afternoon LuAnn looked down from her bedroom window at the familiar figure of Paige Murphey walking by and smiled. That was one determined woman. She wondered, for the thousandth time, what it must be like to be married and expecting a child. It was an experience that was forever out of her reach, and she had long ago reconciled herself to that fact. But that didn't stop her from imagining...

"Enough daydreaming. There's a wedding to plan." Huck looked up from his bed as if to see whether she required an answer from him. Tom ignored her altogether as she closed the door to their top-floor apartments and headed down to the office.

Tess looked up from the desk. "Have you seen Marsha today?"

"She wasn't at breakfast, and I didn't see her at lunch, but then, I don't think I've seen her in a couple of days. She doesn't seem like the type to think wedding planning is fun."

"I don't think so either, but don't lump me in with that grouch."

"Who's a grouch?" Brad stuck his head in the office and grinned. "Hope you weren't talking about me."

"I wasn't," Tess said. "Just talking about the Thornton wedding plans."

He leaned against the doorframe. "Oh? How's everything coming along?"

"We're still on track for the wedding on the afternoon of the sixteenth," LuAnn said.

"Excellent. Actually, I'm here to pick your brain, LuAnn."

"Sure," she said as she followed him out of the office. "What's up?"

He nodded toward the front door. "How about we take a walk? If you have a minute, that is."

LuAnn looked over at Tess, who nodded. "Okay then. Just give me a minute." She hurried upstairs to grab a jacket, then headed down to meet Brad in the lobby.

He was standing at the edge of the café deep in conversation with Taylor when she got to the bottom of the stairs. Doing another heart check, she had to admit he was easy on the eyes. And a truly nice guy, whether he wanted anyone to make a fuss about that or not.

Brad looked up and saw her on the stairs. Giving her a grin and a nod toward the door, he returned his attention to Taylor to shake his hand. When LuAnn joined them, she made sure to thank Taylor for his good work in the inn.

Brad and LuAnn made their way toward the door and stepped out into the sunshine. As they set off down the street, Brad cleared his throat. "As you know, I'm concerned with this growing relationship between your wedding planner and my brother. What do you know about her?"

"Almost nothing, actually. The address on file is in Savannah, Georgia, but Ellie said that address was no longer good since the movers had picked up all her things and were in transit to Marietta."

"If the movers picked up her things, why is she renting a fully furnished house from Justin?"

"Oh." She jolted to a halt and looked at him. "Yes, you're right. I never thought of that until now. Unless she means the things she's moving here are for her wedding planning business. Maybe she has to rent items for Thorn and Bev's wedding because hers are in transit."

"Maybe," he replied.

They walked in companionable silence, stopping occasionally to look in the windows of the shops as they strolled downtown. Brad seemed lost in his own thoughts, leaving LuAnn to allow her mind to go back to the list of wedding tasks awaiting her back at the inn.

"Uncle Brad! Miss LuAnn!"

LuAnn followed the sound to the front door of the Sassy Seamstress where Wendy Wilson, the owner and Grant's other daughter, waved them over. Famous for her quirky sewing-related T-shirts, Wendy was wearing white jeans and a blue top that stated "Yes, I sew. No, I won't hem your pants."

"Do you have a minute?" Wendy called.

Brad looked at LuAnn, and she nodded. "Sure," he said. "Is something wrong?"

She motioned for them to come inside. "I want to show you something."

Stepping into the old building that once housed an eclectic combination of items for sale was like going back to a time when LuAnn's mother used to take her shopping for fabrics. Unlike other girls whose mothers took them to the retail shops to buy clothes, LuAnn's mother bought fabric and made whatever she wore.

The reminder never failed each time she walked into Sassy Seamstress. Oblivious, Brad followed his niece through the wide aisle of materials and quilts up to the old-fashioned counter that was original to the turn-of-the-previous-century building. On the shelves behind the counter were various sewing-related items interspersed with a dozen or so little green frog statues that Grant liked to buy for Wendy as a reminder of his love for her and his desire to make up for not being there when she was growing up.

LuAnn smiled. The pair had certainly come a long way.

The shop was empty, likely because the Monday Lunch Bunch would be showing up to sew in a half hour or so.

Wendy reached under the counter to retrieve an oversized package. Peeling back the paper, she revealed a patchwork quilt made from the most exquisite fabrics LuAnn had ever seen. Rich gold brocade vied with lush scarlet velvet and deepest brown satin shot through with copper threads.

"This is breathtaking," LuAnn whispered as she ran her hand over the detailed stitching that surrounded each square. She returned her attention to Wendy, who now wore a broad grin. "Where did you get this?"

CHAPTER TEN

T hat's an interesting story," Wendy began. "Despite the fact that Barrett George, the former producer of *Quilt Mysteries* and current resident of an Ohio jail, was a total jerk and a lousy boyfriend, I still keep in touch with a couple of the researchers for the show."

LuAnn shook her head as she thought of the popular quilt- and history-themed show that had run on the Arts & Antiques Network for years. If that awful man hadn't been using sweet Wendy for his own evil purposes to find a quilt with ties to her hometown, Marietta and the inn might have been featured. Instead, Wendy got her heart broken, Barrett went to jail, and the show that might have made Wayfarers Inn famous was canceled before filming was complete.

"That's great, sweetheart," Brad said gently. "But what does all of that have to do with this quilt?"

"Well," she said as her grin widened, "one of them contacted me about a month ago to say that she found another quilt with connections to Marietta for sale. She put me in touch with the owner, and I bought it."

"Oh my goodness," LuAnn said. "That's fabulous, and it's a beautiful quilt. The fabric is exquisite, but what's the connection to Marietta?"

Wendy slid a yellowed envelope from the center of the quilt. "Check this out. It's a letter showing who has owned the quilt all the way back to who created it." She paused. "And look at who created it!"

Brad removed a fragile paper from the envelope and set it on the counter between them. "This says this quilt has been in the possession of a family by the name of Inman since 1861. Apparently the current generation wasn't as interested in keeping it as previous ones."

"'A gift to Jefferson Inman from Prudence Willard in honor of Mary,'" LuAnn read and then looked up. "Brad, that's our Prudence! But who is Mary?"

Brad shrugged as he returned the letter to the envelope and handed it back to Wendy. "I guess that's another quilt mystery to be solved someday."

"I know. Isn't it great?" Wendy said.

LuAnn ran her hand across the sumptuous fabric. "These don't look like fabrics that a Quaker woman would wear or even have access to. So Mary must have been a wealthy woman. Perhaps a guest at the inn?"

"It's a mystery, all right. I'm trying to convince my friend at the show to include this in a future episode." Wendy shrugged. "I did mention that they have footage with the inn and its owners that did not have my terrible ex-boyfriend in it, so it would easily transfer to another mystery set here in Marietta."

"Great thinking, Wendy," Brad said as he gave his niece a high five.

"I thought so too." She folded the paper back over the quilt and returned it to its hiding place beneath the counter. "So," she said slowly, "there's another reason I called you over to the shop. It's about my dad."

LuAnn glanced at Brad and met his gaze. "Oh?" she asked. "What about him?"

"Okay. Who is this woman he's seeing? I speak to him almost every day, and I cannot tell you how many 'Ellie' references I've heard since First Friday. Is she as amazing as my father thinks she is, or do we need to stage an intervention?"

Brad chuckled. "I don't think we need to stage an intervention. However, LuAnn and I share your concern."

"Actually, we were just talking about that," LuAnn said. "Neither of us knows much about Ellie, so we are cautiously optimistic about her."

Brad shook his head. "LuAnn, ever the optimist and always a nice person, is cautiously optimistic. I would rather she date someone besides my brother, but I'm going to keep my mouth shut about that for now."

"Well, I'm not," Wendy said. "But don't worry. I won't tell him there are others who agree with me. I guess I'm not so certain. But I'm still going to speak to him." She paused. "He's a grown man, but he's my dad. I don't want him to get his heart broken over some woman who doesn't deserve him."

LuAnn touched Wendy's arm. "Ellie is definitely the friendly type. If she's not serious about your dad, I think he would know that."

The bell on the door jingled, alerting them to a customer's arrival. "Thank you for showing us the quilt," LuAnn said. "It's very exciting. I can't wait to bring Tess and Janice by to see it."

"And thank you for being nice about the lady my father may be dating," Wendy said. She glanced past them and waved. "Hi, hon. Just take a seat and get ready to sew. Let me know if you need any help setting up."

Brad leaned over the counter to wrap his niece in a hug. "I'll do what I can," he told her. "Don't you worry."

Brad and LuAnn made their escape, but not until after three other ladies arrived, each with a sewing machine in tow. Ever chivalrous, Brad held the door open for the women and then helped them select their seats and lift the heavy machines onto the tables.

Exiting quickly to a chorus of thank-yous, Brad joined LuAnn on the sidewalk. "Hurry before more of them show up," he said with a grin.

"You're very popular with the sewing set," she said with a chuckle. "Maybe you should take up sewing."

"No, thanks," he told her. "I'll leave that to others. So, did you mean what you said to Wendy about the possibility that there isn't a romance blooming between Grant and Ellie?"

She sighed. "Maybe. But I don't know for sure, and neither do you."

"All right then," he said as they turned the corner and headed toward the river. "What do you make of that?"

"What?"

LuAnn looked in the direction he was staring. She spied a woman who was most definitely Ellie getting out of a beat-up white car driven by a man who was most definitely *not* Grant.

Ellie glanced over the man's shoulder and waved at them. "Come meet my brother, y'all," she called in an accent that seemed a little thicker than usual.

With Brad leading the way, they closed the distance between them. Her brother? From his dark hair to his bulked-up physique and swarthy skin, he looked absolutely nothing like Ellie.

"Gino is adopted," she said as if reading LuAnn's mind. "He was passing through Marietta on his way home and stopped in to say hello."

After greetings were complete and the brother had shaken their hands with unnecessarily excessive force, Ellie nodded toward the inn. "I suppose I ought to go and check on Marsha. She's been under the weather. I just can't seem to get her interested in doing anything with me these last couple of days."

"That's too bad," LuAnn said. "She hasn't wanted us to come in and change linens or clean either. I hope she doesn't have another migraine."

Ellie shrugged. "Who knows? She's so grumpy all the time anyway that it's impossible to know when she's feeling bad. I'll go and check though."

She turned to Gino and embraced him. "I'm so glad you could stop by this morning. Now you be safe going back home to Savannah."

Brad's eyes narrowed. "Hey, were you at the inn on Friday? You look really familiar."

"Me?" Gino shook his head. "Nah, I don't go for artsy things." It didn't take a sleuth to notice the muscle man's laughter held more than a slight edge of anxiety. He swiped at his dark curls with his palm and shrugged.

Ellie poked him in the arm. "Don't you need to get going?"

"Oh, sure, yeah. Later," he said to her before he turned his attention to LuAnn and then to Brad. "Nice to meet you two." He got in his car.

"And you," LuAnn said.

He started the car and shifted into gear. "Later," he said again to Ellie, who responded with a wave as he drove off in a cloud of exhaust fumes.

Ellie turned to walk toward the inn without looking back. Brad grasped LuAnn's elbow to stop her from following. "What was that all about, do you think?"

LuAnn pursed her lips. "I have no idea. I sure am ready for some answers instead of so many questions though."

"Did you notice that Gino guy knew about First Friday even though Ellie clearly said he was just passing through?"

"Maybe Ellie told him about it."

Brad looked doubtful. "It's possible," he said slowly. "But he does look a lot like the guy I saw at the inn. Didn't you notice him?"

"I was too busy making sure everything was going as planned," she said. "I spoke to a lot of people, but there were so many I didn't recognize." She paused. "Tess has said from the beginning that there is something just not right about Ellie and Marsha. I'm beginning to agree."

Brad gave her a sideways look. "Uh-oh. Is there a mystery in the works?"

She groaned. "More than one, I'm afraid. There's still the issue with the food trucks, remember?"

"Did you solve it?" he asked.

"No, and I saw another one parked outside the inn recently. A different one."

"You know," Brad said, "there was some talk at the last city council meeting about a parcel of land not too far from the inn being zoned commercial and turned into a food truck park. My recollection is the decision was tabled for approval at the April meeting. Maybe these guys are coming to scope it out."

LuAnn grinned. "Oh, I bet you're right. That would certainly explain it. Still, it doesn't explain why they drove off so rapidly."

"I guess that's another mystery," he said.

"I agree. As for Ellie, maybe she's not such a mystery after all." At Brad's doubtful expression, LuAnn continued. "I think we're all going to find out eventually that our wedding planner is just a flirt who likes to socialize." She paused. "And truly, I don't think she and Grant will end up in any sort of relationship. My guess is Ellie likes playing the field far too much."

"And so does my brother," Brad said. "Although he's getting older, so who knows?"

"We all are," LuAnn said. "But that's neither here nor there. How about we go back to the inn, and I buy you a cup of coffee? If you don't have any plans this evening, Winnie is testing a brand-new soup that we're having for supper tonight."

He laughed. "Much as I would love that, I've got an appointment that I need to be heading toward soon."

"Oh," she said as brightly as she could manage. "All right then."

"Rain check?" he said, his blue eyes shining and that dimple bolstered by a dazzling smile.

"Of course."

She walked as far as the inn's front door with him, then paused when he once again reached for her elbow. "LuAnn, I just want to thank you for being a good friend. Not just to me but to my niece. I really appreciate you."

She smiled. "I am very happy to be your friend, Brad," she told him sincerely.

He smiled and seemed to want to say more. Then, with a nod, he took off toward his car.

LuAnn stepped inside the inn to find the whole place in an uproar. She didn't have to guess twice to know who was at the center of it.

May 4, 1860

Once Moses had been fed and tucked into his blankets, Prudence prepared a meal for Jason and herself. When it was ready, she stepped out onto the porch to call her husband to the table but found only his Bible there.

"Jason," she called when she determined he was nowhere near the house. "Husband?" she added. "Where has thee gone? Thy dinner is ready."

"Over here," he called from the direction of the river. "We shall be there directly."

We? Prudence picked up the Bible and leaned against the doorframe to slow her racing heart. Had the stranger her husband told her about earlier already found them?

A moment later, Jason appeared on the path walking slowly alongside a man of approximately thirty years, give or take. The fellow wore spectacles on his abundant nose and had a shock of red curls that were poorly covered by his hat. The remainder of his outfit, a formal-looking dark frock coat and trousers, looked more suited to a banker's office than the rough terrain of the river path.

Prudence stepped down from the porch to meet them, the Bible tucked under her arm. "Welcome," she told the stranger.

"Prudence," Jason said, "this is Professor Rhett Ashworth. He teaches geology at the college."

The professor offered a broad smile. "I like to think I just study rocks. And I am very pleased to meet you, Mrs. Willard. Your husband speaks very highly of you."

Prudence felt heat climb into her cheeks. "As I would speak very highly of him," she responded.

"And I as well," he agreed. "Your husband was invaluable to our team these past few days. Thank you for loaning him to us."

Prudence exchanged a look with Jason. "I hardly can take credit. Chasing after the meteorites was an idea that came from him alone."

"The professor and I are like-minded on many subjects," Jason said.

"Indeed we are." Professor Ashworth looked past them to smile. "Is that a tame goose?"

Glancing around, Prudence spied Patience waddling toward them. As the noisy bird moved closer, Prudence realized she was silent when the sight of a stranger would normally cause uncontrollable honking of the most annoying sort.

Then she spied the reason why. Patience was carrying the meteorite in her bill. She dropped the chunk of rock at Prudence's feet, then began her usual honking.

"Hush now," Prudence told the goose as she knelt down to retrieve the rock and return it to Jason.

"A pity we did not have that goose with us in New Concord," Professor Ashworth said with a grin. "Imagine the time we would have saved if we could have sent a dozen like that one out to fetch the rocks for us."

"We've despaired of training her," Prudence said. "Although our son seems to get her to do his bidding with no effort."

"Your son must be a clever trainer of animals, then," he said.

Jason laughed. "Our son is but a year old."

"Ah." The professor smiled. "Then he is an early learner. I suspect I shall see him at the college before long."

Jason smiled also. "Prudence and I had this conversation today, actually. So, yes, perhaps someday." He nodded toward the farmhouse. "Won't you come inside and finish our conversation there?"

Prudence allowed a moment of panic. The food she'd prepared was sufficient for her and Jason but only just. She pasted on a smile and sent a prayer skyward. There would be enough. With the Lord there always was. Then there was the other thing that troubled her, namely, the evening's upcoming delivery.

"Yes, won't you come in? I've just set a place at the table."

"How did you do that?" the professor asked. "I almost assuredly arrived unannounced."

"I suppose I just knew," she said. "Now please, come and enjoy."

Prudence placed the Bible on Jason's chair and tucked the rock into her pocket. Her fingers grazed the ribbon, and she tucked it deeper below the meteorite fragment.

Though the professor made a fuss about not interrupting dinner, he finally gave in and accepted their hospitality. Prudence served the men, and then offered a broad smile.

"Now please excuse me. I dined earlier with our son, so I will allow you men your conversation."

Jason opened his mouth to protest, but Prudence moved out of their guest's line of sight and shook her head. She had indeed finished the few bites of the food left on her son's plate while she was preparing Jason's meal. So indeed, if the facts were not examined too closely, she had dined earlier.

But the truth was she could not have managed a bite of food knowing there was a stranger in her home and two packages being delivered shortly. The two persons who would be escaping an impossible life to freedom should not be put off by a social call from a teacher of the study of rocks.

CHAPTER ELEVEN

How could Marsha just disappear?" LuAnn asked Ellie as she comforted her on the settee in the fourth-floor apartment. When she'd walked in the door, Ellie was wailing about her missing companion, so LuAnn had taken on the task of comforting her while Tess phoned the police.

She had escorted the distraught woman upstairs to the Inn Crowd's shared living area and settled her down with a cup of chamomile tea. Now to talk some sense into her and, just possibly, get some information that might be useful in finding the missing Marsha.

"Surely it isn't possible for her to just disappear into thin air, considering the way you two are practically joined at the hip."

"I know," Ellie said, her mascara running and tears flowing. "But we'd had a bit of a falling-out before she took to her room. I don't like to speak ill of her, but Marsha isn't the easiest person to get along with."

"Well, don't worry. Tess is downstairs calling the police now. They'll make sure she's found."

"Police? No! She absolutely cannot call the police!"

Ellie jumped up from the settee and ran out of the room so fast that Tom jerked awake and hissed at her. Huck went racing after the frantic blonde, likely thinking a game of chase was on.

LuAnn hurried to try to catch the pup before he managed to arrive on the first floor.

Unfortunately, Ellie was much more nimble than LuAnn anticipated. Not only did she beat them all to the first floor, but she raced to the check-in desk like her skirts were on fire, yelling incoherently. Warming to the game, Huck began to bark. LuAnn lunged for the dog but missed and tripped on the last three stairs, managing to land on her feet.

"Impressive, Miss LuAnn," Taylor said as he handed the guilty-looking pup to her. "I'd say that was a solid 'ten'—for your age bracket."

"Ha, ha, very funny." She grinned at him, hefted the little dog onto her shoulder, and limped around the corner.

Tess came running around the check-in desk and slammed into Ellie, who backed up, then dodged her and snatched the phone cord out of the wall. At the same time, the kitchen door opened and Winnie stood there like a queen holding her wooden spoon scepter high.

"What in the world is going on out here?"

By the time an officer arrived to take their statements, Janice and LuAnn had managed to get Ellie calmed down. The poor young man was apparently new to the force, as witnessed by his shiny badge, his look of confusion, and his apparent age.

Had she seen Officer Blair Goggan walking down the street, LuAnn would have assumed he was a teenager. Evidently he was old enough to graduate from the police academy, or at least she hoped he was.

The officer had them all move to the kitchen and take places around the table.

"What I don't understand," he said, "is why Miss Miller would want to disable the inn's telephone."

Ellie affected a much put-upon expression, and then smiled. "It was all a tremendous misunderstanding." She dabbed at her eyes with a tissue as she glanced around the room and then back at the officer. "I'm very distraught because my dearest friend and cousin is missing. Of course."

"Of course," he echoed.

LuAnn couldn't think of anything she had seen or heard in the past few days that even came close to suggesting that Ellie and Marsha were friends, much less "dearest" friends. But she kept that to herself.

"Why, it's just too much. I got overexcited, I guess you'd say, and then when I heard you would be called, well, that was just too much."

He lifted one dark brow. "And why is that?"

"Well, to have the police called, that just made it all too…" She paused as if having difficulty speaking. "Too real," she managed as the waterworks began again.

"There, there, Miss Miller," he said as he allowed the crying woman to lean forward and rest her head on his shoulder, smearing mascara on his dark gray shirt. "I promise to muster the entire force of officers here in Marietta if that is what it takes to find your cousin."

At that, Ellie let out a wail. Winnie stood, rolled her eyes, and went back to her soup pot.

"I wasn't even going to use that phone to call the police," Tess said evenly.

Ellie's crying ceased, and she turned toward Tess. "You weren't? How else were you going to call them?"

Tess held up her cell phone and waved it. "Uh…with this?"

Ellie's mascara-smudged eyes narrowed. "How was I supposed to know you would call with a cell phone? This is a fancy inn, so I just assumed you would have a fancy phone to go with your fancy inn. So excuse me for assuming you would be that fancy."

"Fancy," Tess echoed with a grin that held no humor. "Right, okay."

"Now, ladies," Officer Goggan said. "There is no need to add to the upset."

"She started it," Ellie said. "I am merely grieving a loved one, but she is—"

"All right, look here," Winnie said, calling them all to attention. "There is no need to speak that way, young lady," she said to Ellie. "You have been flouncing around here acting like everything related to you is the most important thing in the world. Well, let me tell you that if your cousin is missing, that ought to be what counts."

Ellie froze. Then she slowly straightened and dabbed at the dark circles on the officer's shirt before wiping her eyes. The transformation from broken woman to defiant female was stunning. She looked at Officer Goggan. "If you'll excuse me, please, Officer, I would like to take a break to freshen up. I will return shortly." She turned her back on all of them and walked out of the kitchen as if she were a model strutting down the runway in a fashion show.

Winnie shook her head once the door closed behind Ellie, then went back to the soup she had been stirring.

Tess rose. "I've got work to do in the office. If you need me, Officer Goggan, that's where you can find me."

He nodded his permission, and she left the kitchen.

Janice wandered over to consult with Winnie on the soup, leaving LuAnn and Taylor at the table. "I ought to get back to work, don't you think?" Taylor said.

"Yes, go ahead," LuAnn told him. "If Officer Goggan needs a statement, he'll know where to find you."

Taylor shrugged. "I don't have much of a statement. I never saw the missing lady come in or go out while I was on duty. Just Ellie."

"Do you remember the last time you saw the missing woman?" the officer asked him.

"I'd guess it was Friday, a few hours before the event. She and Ellie were having an argument about something. I didn't pay much attention, because I was busy."

"Thank you," Officer Goggan said. "I'll let you know if I have any more questions."

He turned to LuAnn and Janice. "What about you two? When did you last see the missing woman?"

They exchanged glances, and LuAnn shrugged. "I saw her Saturday morning. They were coming back from looking at houses with Grant. Marsha was fussing at Ellie, but that's how they always were. That's my last memory of seeing her."

Janice nodded. "I saw them go in their rooms when they got back. My recollection is the same—they were arguing. I haven't seen her since then."

Officer Goggan made a few more notes, then returned his notepad to his pocket.

"Would you like some soup, Officer?" Winnie called. "Janice and I are trying out a new recipe before we present it in the café and could use your opinion."

He gave her a doubtful look.

"Go ahead," LuAnn encouraged. "I speak from experience when I say that it may take Ellie a while to reapply her makeup and return for questioning."

Officer Goggan grinned. "Then I would love to. Thank you, ma'am," he said to Winnie. "My mother brings home soup from here all the time, so I am well acquainted with the current menu."

"Is that right?" Winnie asked. "Who's your mama? I bet I know her."

As the pair settled into a comfortable conversation, LuAnn leaned toward Janice. "I'll go up and check on Ellie. We don't have hours to just sit here. I've still got a florist to call and a hundred other details to go over with the future Mr. and Mrs. Thornton and Laura before the end of the day."

"Go ahead," Janice said with a sweep of her hand. "If they need you, I'll text."

"Thanks." She slipped off her stool and headed for the door just as Winnie poured a ladle of soup into a bowl and handed it to the officer. "I'll be right back," she told them as the door closed behind her.

She climbed the stairs and then paused a moment before knocking at Ellie's door. "Ellie?" she called. "It's time to finish up and come downstairs."

No response.

"Ellie?"

Again, nothing. LuAnn reached for the knob and turned it. The door opened just enough for her to call out, "Ellie? Are you in here? The officer is waiting for you to finish talking to him."

She gave the door a push and stepped inside Apples and Cinnamon. The room looked like someone had torn through the place with the intent to destroy everything in sight. Every dresser drawer was open, and clothing had been strewn from one end of the room to the other.

A suitcase had been upended on the bed, and a pile of shoes spilled out from beneath the blankets. Ellie's oversized purse was upside down, the contents scattered on the floor, and a lamp was turned over onto a pillow.

The room looked like a crime scene.

"Oh no!" LuAnn's heart lurched. She took a step backward and retrieved her phone to call Janice. "Send Officer Goggan up to Apples and Cinnamon. I think something has happened to Ellie."

"He's on his way up," Janice said.

LuAnn replaced the phone in her pocket and waited at the door until the policeman arrived with Janice on his heels. "I only touched the doorknob," she told him. "I've solved enough mysteries to know you're not supposed to disturb the crime scene."

He gave her a curt nod and motioned for her to clear the doorway. "I'll handle this."

Picking his way through the mess with an agility befitting his youth, Officer Goggan stopped in front of the closed bathroom door. Slowly, he turned the knob.

Then came the scream.

Officer Goggan went down when a blur of white fell on top of him. A moment later, Ellie climbed to her feet, a towel hanging askew atop her head. Her face was smeared with some sort of white cream.

"What in the world? Are you people crazy?" she screamed. She clutched her bathrobe to her chest. "Can't a woman get herself pretty without her privacy being invaded?"

The officer climbed to his feet and retrieved his hat from the floor. "I'm terribly sorry," he mumbled as he made his way back out the door, pressing past LuAnn and out of the room.

Janice went in to calm the frantic woman while LuAnn caught up with Officer Goggan. "I'm so sorry. With what that room looked like, I thought for sure there had been foul play."

He dusted off his pants. "I did too. When she jumped out of the bathroom wearing that white stuff on her face and that towel on her head, I thought I'd seen a ghost." He looked down at his shirt, now streaked with whatever white substance Ellie had been wearing. "Now it looks like the ghost rubbed off on me."

A laugh bubbled up, and LuAnn gave in to it. A moment later, Officer Goggan joined her, and then they were both laughing uncontrollably. Finally, LuAnn sobered enough to nod toward Marsha's suite.

"Would you like to take a look at the missing woman's room? She declined service for the last few days, and as far as I know, no one from the staff has gone in since Friday morning, so you may find some clues." She paused. "Unless it looks like Ellie's room, in which case, I don't know what you'll find."

"I think that's a good idea. And speaking of, you can tell Miss Miller I will take her statement down at the station when she's ready to give it."

"Don't want to go back in there?" she asked with a grin.

"Ma'am," he said slowly as he used the tissue she handed him to dab at his shirt, "I haven't been on the force long, but I have seen my share of crime scenes. That room takes the cake. But we may need to do a thorough investigation and process the scene. It's possible this happened while the lady was bathing."

"I suppose that's true." She thought of the telephone wire escapade. "I'm afraid we're going to have to pay the staff extra to clean it when you're done."

He grimaced. "I hope you've got deep pockets."

"No, but we've got really nice employees," she said.

"All right. Then let's see if this room is anything like her friend's."

"Cousin," LuAnn corrected.

"Great. A relative. Well, okay, here goes nothing." Using his tissue, Officer Goggan opened the door and stepped inside.

CHAPTER TWELVE

In stark contrast to Ellie's room, Marsha had left Moonlight and Snowflakes spotless. Officer Goggan picked his way carefully around the bed and poked his head into the closet before moving to the bathroom.

After looking around in there for a few minutes, he went to the window and looked out. Then he tried to lift the sash.

"We keep them locked, but they do open," LuAnn said.

Continuing his investigation, he lifted the bed skirt, looked underneath, and then went around and did the same on the other side. He picked up each pillow, then went to the desk and checked inside the drawer.

Finally, he straightened and turned to face LuAnn. "This room is spotless. I wonder if you might tell me just what sort of woman this Marsha is, because I can tell you one thing. She's quite the housekeeper compared to her cousin across the hall."

"I'm really not sure of much about her other than the name she gave when she checked in." LuAnn shrugged. "She was grumpy almost every time I saw her, but now that I've had the opportunity to be around Ellie for a few days, I can't say I blame her for having that attitude."

Office Goggan nodded. "I'd be grumpy too." He paused. "For that matter, I'd probably be ready to bolt and run, which begs the question of whether that may be what happened here. Do you think that's possible?"

"That she would leave without telling Ellie?" LuAnn thought about their behavior the last time she saw them together and nodded. "Given what I've seen, yes, that's possible."

"Do you have an address for her?" he asked. "Maybe a phone number? This whole thing may be resolved with just a phone call."

"I don't, but I'm sure Ellie does. She is her cousin after all." LuAnn led him back out into the hallway. Sounds of Janice's calming tone and Ellie's screech echoed in the enclosed space.

Officer Goggan grimaced. "I'm not looking forward to that interview."

"I don't blame you," she said.

He followed her downstairs, then ducked into the kitchen while LuAnn paused at the door to Tess's office. "Well?" Tess asked. "What was all the excitement up there?"

"Ellie, of course." LuAnn leaned against the doorframe. "I noticed you didn't come running up there. Everything okay?"

Tess nodded. "I handled a few calls from wedding vendors. They're on board for the sixteenth."

"Okay then." LuAnn sighed. "At least something positive happened this afternoon."

Tess grinned at the sound of Winnie's laughter floating across from the kitchen. A moment later, the officer came out with a large container of soup.

"For my mom," he told them as he hurried toward the front door.

Winnie came out a step behind him. "He's a nice young man," she said. "His mama is the daughter of an old friend of mine. I cannot believe that child is old enough to have a child old enough to be a police officer. How time does fly." She glanced up at the stairs and then back at Tess and LuAnn. "So what was all the commotion up there about? Is that woman still causing trouble?"

LuAnn sighed. "You have no idea."

Winnie rolled her eyes. "I can handle this if you want me to. That girl just needs someone to tell her to grow up and act right."

"If only it were so simple," Tess said.

"Oh, it is simple," Winnie answered. "Trouble is, some people just don't want to hear it. I figure that one up there for either a spoiled brat or a really good actress."

"That's it," Tess exclaimed.

"What?" LuAnn asked.

"She's an actress. Maybe they're both actresses. Remember that woman who was pretending to be an antiques dealer? She stayed at the inn and acted like she was scouting for furniture when she was really scouting for a movie location."

"Dear Fiona," LuAnn said. "Yes, that's true. But what makes you think that about Ellie?"

"That's easy." Tess shook her head. "For one thing, she's such a diva. It's really over the top, don't you think? Then there's the fact she claims to be a wedding planner, but you seem to be doing all the work."

LuAnn considered the question. "You could be right. She said that she was used to the finer things, while Marsha was raised in the country without those privileges, but she sure didn't sound refined when she was screeching about our 'fancy' inn."

"I'd say screeching is an understatement. I think what she actually did was break character." Tess shrugged. "I think the real question in all of this is why. What do you think, Winnie?"

Winnie rested one hand on her hip and shrugged. "Only reason anyone ever does something like that is because they want something. Now what you ought to be asking is what she wants."

"You're a wise woman," Tess said. "I vote we go ask right now."

"I don't think that's a good idea," LuAnn said. "Trust me on this. It would be best to wait and let her calm down before you try to ask her anything."

"I agree," Janice said from the stairs. "I finally got her to sit down and take a deep breath, but that woman is wound tighter than a grandfather clock right now."

"I am impressed," LuAnn said. "But where in the world did she find someplace to sit down?"

Tess looked over at her. "What do you mean?"

"Well," Janice said as she joined them, "let's just say that LuAnn thought there had been a crime committed in that room."

LuAnn laughed as she described the scene she had encountered in Apples and Cinnamon. "Then there was the issue of the face cream all over poor Officer Goggan."

"So that's what that white stuff was. I thought it was frosting, but I never got a chance to ask where he ran into it."

"Actually, it ran into him," LuAnn said with a chuckle.

"Oh, I have got to hear this," Winnie said, "but I have something on the stove. Come back in the kitchen and tell us the whole story, and don't leave out a detail."

By the time LuAnn finished the tale, Winnie had supplied them all with bowls of the soup she had been experimenting with as well as slices of sourdough bread warm from the oven.

Robin walked in a little while later and stopped short. "It looks like the party started without me," she said. "I knew there was a reason I stayed late today."

"Come on and join us," Winnie told her. "Tess was just telling me about how your paycheck was going to be a little bigger this time because she's got a special project she needs help with."

"Should I be happy about this?" Robin asked.

They all laughed, and Robin shook her head. "What has that woman in Apples and Cinnamon done this time?"

Winnie grinned. "It's a long story, but I've got soup and fresh bread. Sit a spell."

"Someone else is going to have to tell it this time," LuAnn said. "I really need to get back to working on the wedding plans."

"Isn't that Ellie's job?" Robin asked as she slathered butter on a warm slice of bread.

"She's saving that for later," Janice said with a grin. "Now is not a good time."

"This is where I came in." LuAnn rose, picked up her bowl and spoon, and took them over to the sink to wash them. "I'm going to leave this story for the rest of you to tell."

When the door closed behind her a few minutes later, Janice and Tess were telling their versions of the story while Robin was laughing so hard she could barely eat her soup. Winnie stood regally by and added her opinion when she felt it was necessary.

Though she hated to leave the fun, LuAnn knew she had already allowed more diversions into her day than she should have. She went into her sitting room to call Beverly and update her on the arrangements she had made with the florist. "We haven't had a chance to talk about food," she said, "but I think that's going to be the next decision to make since we only have a short amount of time to get it settled. Unless Ellie has already discussed this with you."

"LuAnn, whatever you decide is going to be great with Thorn and me."

"But don't you want to have some input? I mean, what if Ellie or I choose something that you hate? Now, that would ruin a wedding."

Beverly laughed. "Look, why don't you just talk to Laura? She's the one who wanted this wedding. I would rather be surprised, and I know Thorn would too."

"Are you sure?"

"I am absolutely sure. And honey, please convey my thanks to that wedding planner lady and whoever else has been helping you. I never thought I would be having a real wedding, much less one so nice."

"We're going to try to make it extra special."

LuAnn spent the next half hour going over ideas with Laura and making notes to give to Ellie. When she finally hung up and finalized her notes, the clock read half past seven.

"Goodness, Huck," she said as she scratched the dog behind his ears. "Where is the time going? Come on, let's take you for a quick walk before we settle in for the night."

Huck jumped down and raced to the spot where his leash was kept and waited patiently while LuAnn attached it. After a long walk and plenty of time barking at anything that moved in the thicket along the river, Huck tugged at the leash to head back toward the inn.

"Too chilly for you out here?" she said as she shrugged deeper into her jacket. "I should have put you in your sweater."

The pup wagged his tail and barked in response. "Well then," she said. "If that's how you feel, then let's go home."

When LuAnn got back to her rooms, she discovered she was all wedding planned out for the day. She wasn't quite ready to go to bed, so she decided to take the time to transfer the pictures she took Friday night from her camera to her computer. She clicked through them, pleased. She'd done her best to get a picture of just about everyone there, and some of them were really quite good. Thirty minutes later she closed her laptop, unable to stop yawning. She sat on her bed and picked up the photo frame that held her father's picture and ran her fingers around the edge. She felt the prayer that always came to her when she thought of him, a thankfulness mixed with a longing that no words could express.

Word must have gotten out the next day about Winnie's new soup, because there was standing room only in the café for lunch. After the kitchen was finally clean, LuAnn took Huck for another spin around the neighborhood. The crisp March air revived her spirits and cleared her mind.

"Hi, LuAnn!"

She looked around to see Paige walking toward her at a brisk pace. "No baby yet?"

"Not yet," Paige said as she continued past her. "But I'm hopeful. The doctor says keep walking, so I'm walking."

"Good luck," she called to Paige's retreating back.

Back up in the apartment, she poured fresh water in Huck's and Tom's bowls and fed them both. As the two unlikely furry friends dined on their kibble, LuAnn made a cup of tea. Finally she was ready to go down and tackle the conversation with Ellie.

Tucking the notebook under her arm, LuAnn closed the door behind her, walked down one flight of stairs, and turned toward Apples and Cinnamon. Ellie answered on the first knock with a smile on her face.

"Do come in," she said. "I was hoping you'd come visit, or else I was going to have to try to find you."

"I came to talk about the Thornton wedding. What did you need me for?"

She stopped short. While the room was not immaculate, it was close. The dresser drawers were all closed, the bed was made, and there wasn't a single piece of clothing littering the bed or the floor. The suitcases that had been strewn about were now neatly stacked in the corner, and the white robe that had frightened Officer Goggan was draped across the chair.

"Oh my goodness," she said. "Robin definitely deserves that bonus."

"Who is Robin?"

"The woman who works for us." LuAnn gave another sweeping glance, and then returned her attention to Ellie. "She's the one who was sent to clean up the mess that was left after the police left."

Ellie affected a haughty look. LuAnn immediately thought of Tess's claim that she and her supposed cousin were playing roles.

"So that's who kept trying to get in here," she said. "I told her to come back later, but she wouldn't listen. It took me telling sweet Janice that I was busy cleaning up to get her to leave. I do like Janice."

"Yes, Janice is wonderful." LuAnn shook her head. "So you cleaned all this up?"

"It may surprise you, given the fact that I am now a successful wedding planner, but there was a time when I made my living cleaning houses. So yes, I cleaned all this up."

"Well," LuAnn managed, "that is impressive. And now that you've mentioned wedding planning, I really need to talk to you about the Thorntons. I spoke with their daughter, Laura, and she has some definite ideas about what she wants."

"Wonderful," Ellie said. "Why don't you leave your notes, and I will look over them."

"I, um, well..." LuAnn clutched her notebook to her chest. "I'd really much rather talk to you about it."

"Maybe we could do that a little later. I was about to go out to check on the florist. Has he okayed our requests?"

"Yes, he has. I'm going to go over there tomorrow to make sure we're on the same page." LuAnn glanced at her watch and then back at Ellie.

"I can go now. I don't mind."

LuAnn shook her head. "No, really. Tomorrow is fine. Now let's talk about what Laura would like for her parents."

"Really, LuAnn," Ellie said. "I really can't right now. All this cleaning has exhausted me."

"Really, Ellie," LuAnn echoed. "If you had the energy to go to the florist, then you have the energy to talk to me." She sighed. "But I do have a few things I need to do in the office downstairs for a while. Do you think you can be rested enough in about an hour to talk about the wedding plans?"

Ellie's smile dripped with honey. "I think that will be just fine." She stretched her arms over her head and yawned. "I'll just lie down for a bit. Do you want me to come downstairs to you, or would you like to meet up here? Whatever is convenient for you is just fine with me."

LuAnn spoke through a tight smile. "I'll come back up here. See you in an hour." She turned and headed for the stairs. *Oh, Marsha, where did you go? And can I come too?*

Chapter Thirteen

May 4, 1860

As the minutes ticked by and then half an hour passed, Prudence watched the shadows lengthen outside. The men were deep in conversation with no sign of slowing. She heard bits of a discussion about aerolites, talk of how early to plant a fall garden, and debate regarding the proper way to snatch honeycomb from a hive without being stung.

Moses began to whimper, and she went in to soothe him. As her palm rested gently on the little boy's back, she offered a silent prayer that the Lord would be with them all tonight, but especially with those two souls who would find freedom once the night fell.

She remained with her son until the worry bubbled up, and she could no longer keep still and silent. Likely sensing her mood, Moses wiggled and threatened to awaken.

Prudence tucked the blanket up around him and tiptoed out of the room. The time for the meeting at the river was drawing near. Whether the professor was still under her roof or not, she must leave soon.

Stepping out of the dimly lit room, she blinked to adjust her eyes to the lamplight. The men had adjourned to the porch, where their voices were reduced to deep murmurs punctuated with soft laughter.

She walked over to retrieve Jason's Bible and tried to read to pass the time. After a while, when Prudence realized she had read the same passage of Isaiah three times, she gave up the effort. The time to leave was upon her.

Prudence dug into her pocket and retrieved the ribbon, then folded it into Jason's Bible. Returning the book to her husband's chair, she took her cloak from the peg and slipped out the back door into the deepening darkness.

As the lights of the farmhouse faded behind her, the night sounds rose. Off in the distance the soft lap of water against the bank provided the only indication that the river was up ahead. She followed the path more by memory than by sight as she slowly made her way toward the place where the boat would be hidden.

With the moon nearly full, the water shimmered silver as Prudence stepped out of the thicket and onto the riverbank. She looked to the right and then to the left, but the boat was nowhere in sight.

Prudence stepped back into the thicket, her heart pounding. Had the location of the meeting changed? At the splash of oars slapping against water, she ducked out of sight.

Scraping sounds nearby echoed through the night air alerting her to the nearness of the boat. She moved through the thicket until she could see the source of the sound.

There was a boat right where the one she was to meet should have been. But where was the person who had landed it in that spot?

Prudence froze, then slowly allowed her gaze to scan the forest around her. Seeing nothing and no one, she moved closer, remaining in the thicket rather than showing herself on the riverbank. Something rustled behind her, and she jumped to turn toward the sound but saw nothing.

How long she sat crouched in the thicket, Prudence couldn't say. Surely by now whoever had taken the boat and returned it was long gone. Something crawled across her arm, and she swatted at it as the chilly night air settled into her bones.

Finally certain she was alone, Prudence rose to ease her aching legs, and then took a tentative step forward toward the riverbank. Eventually she reached the edge of the thicket. The next step would bring her into the open on the sandy bank.

Peering out from behind a tree, all she saw was the boat and the river beyond. Though her heart pounded, and everything in her said to stay right where she was, Prudence stepped out onto the riverbank and walked slowly toward the vessel that would take her to the other side of the river.

To fail tonight would mean the possible loss of two lives, so she cast her fear away and tried to imagine the faces of the ones she would be bringing to freedom. There had been so many over the years since she joined the effort here in Marietta, so many whose lives had been changed by people who cared enough to set their fears aside and do what was right. What was terrifying.

Whispering a prayer with each step, Prudence climbed into the boat and reached for the oar. Only then did she realize she was not alone.

A scream died in her throat as the shadowy figure of a man sprang up from the depths of the vessel to press his palm over her mouth. She fought him until spots appeared in front of her eyes.

"Stop." She heard a voice that should not have been near. "We are on the same side."

She froze. Though her mind still reeled with questions, she ceased her fight.

"Will you not cause us to be heard, please?" Slowly she nodded, relaxed, at least for the moment.

The hand came away from her mouth. "I assume you have questions, as do I," Professor Ashworth said softly. "Now is not the time. We have two lives at stake, and I am not referring to our own."

"Where is my husband?" she demanded.

"Likely wondering where his wife has gone off to." He stood to reach one leg over and shove the boat back into the water, then took his seat and reached for the oars. "Unless you told him."

"I hadn't the chance," she said as she thought of the ribbon hidden in his Bible. "Though he may know by now."

With a curt nod, the professor set a course for the Virginia side of the river. Prudence gripped the sides of the boat until her hands ached while questions tormented her. Finally she could stand it no more.

"Did thee know of me and my association?" she asked him, unwilling to admit just yet that Jason was also involved in activities of the Underground Railroad.

He met her gaze but said nothing for a moment. "Your husband and I discovered by accident that we had certain friends in common. Later we learned that his invitation to New Concord was not by chance."

"I did wonder, given Jason's infirmities..." She paused, refusing to speak ill of her husband or to cast any negative light on him. "He does not have the ability to walk as far as some, and I did wonder why he was chosen when many others might have been more fit for the task."

The professor nodded. "I see what you mean, but I assure you that was not a concern. You see, there are many of us here in Ohio and elsewhere, but as you know, we rarely speak of what we do, and often one does not know the other when passing him on the street."

At her silence, he continued. "Marietta College has become a stop on the railroad. Perhaps you didn't know. There are others who think as your husband and I do, but for the sake of our employment and the work we do with the railroad, we cannot speak out."

She knew there were other places in Marietta and nearby besides the Riverfront House where travelers were housed on their way north. Most were private homes, but others hid escapees in attics or upper floors of businesses right in town.

For safety's sake, the locations of these places were only known to a few.

"So when two men should be introduced because they might have help to offer one another, the Lord often orchestrates a reason for that to occur."

"That He does," she admitted.

The sound of the oars slipping through the water seemed magnified here at the center of the river. Though the professor did not seem like a man of strength, his ability to row the boat against the current had brought them this far swiftly.

"You still do not trust me." The moon slanted silver light across his face, casting his features in shadow.

"I believe thee would agree I have yet not had sufficient time to decide."

"Thus you are not yet comfortable with sharing this vessel with me."

"Or this mission," she said. "Not yet. No."

With a nod, Professor Ashworth agreed. "And that is fair. Had I not spent time with your husband—who is a fine and hardworking man—I would feel the same about sharing this vessel with you."

She managed a smile at the mention of Jason. "I will agree with your assessment of my husband."

"Something we do have in common. There were other men on our expedition to New Concord who would also agree. I am hopeful that I can introduce him to my friend who happened upon the meteorite event while taking photographs at…"

Professor Ashworth's words faded as Prudence caught sight of movement on the shore. She froze even as the professor turned and searched for what had captured her attention.

"There," he said. "I see our charges. Hold on while I make for shore."

The boat lurched forward, and they were soon at the opposite bank. Three figures slipped from the thicket.

"There were to be but two," Professor Ashworth protested. "I don't like this. It would not be the first time that an unexpected person turned out to be working for the slave owners. Watch carefully, and prepare to take cover if I have to use my weapon."

Prudence gave silent assent.

"Why three?" the professor called out in a voice just loud enough for the strangers to hear. "We were told two."

A man of advanced age hobbled forward, the moonlight showing his features clearly. "Please, sir," he said, his voice unsteady, "if I am to choose between my grandson and my granddaughter, then take them both, and leave me here. I am Amos. This is Thomas, and this is Mary."

The old man's expression begged, but his posture held straight and proud. The two standing behind him held tight to one another but said nothing.

"There is no need for choice tonight, sir," the professor said as he held the boat still while motioning for Prudence to help the passengers aboard. "There is room for all three of you. I am more than happy to bring you across the river to safety, but I am curious how there came to be one more than expected."

Amos was the last to be seated, seeing first to his granddaughter and then his grandson. "I was told my granddaughter was gone forever."

The old man looked away. For a moment, silence filled the air.

Amos continued. "I used to hate it when people would talk all around me as if I wasn't there. As if I wasn't human." He paused. "Now, I am grateful for that treatment, as it might have saved a life. Maybe all three of our lives."

Prudence's attention swung to the beautiful young girl now seated beside her. Unlike the men who wore the rough garments of a field hand, Mary was dressed in a gown of breathtaking quality and style. Even in the moonlight Prudence could see that gold brocade and lace vied with lush scarlet velvet on the skirt, and the bodice was made of deepest brown satin shot through with copper threads. The dress was threadbare in some places but beautiful all the same.

"Had I not been treated this way on this particular afternoon, I might not have known that my granddaughter was close by." Amos reached across to grasp Mary's hand. "I am thankful to the Lord for these mercies He has shown me and my family."

The young man beside him—a handsome fellow of no more than fifteen or sixteen years—looked away, his expression grim. Anger etched his features and showed in his clenched fists as he made a sound of derision when the Lord's name was mentioned.

Professor Ashworth paused his rowing to address the boy. "You are safe now, Thomas," he said. "Your escape is complete. See, we are nearing the banks. You'll be safe at the college until arrangements can be made for your journey north."

"You mistake the cause of his anger. Thomas is here against his will," Amos said. "Had I not reminded him that an old man and a girl need the protection of a man of his strength and abilities, Thomas would have preferred to stay behind."

"Whatever for?" Prudence blurted out. "I cannot feature a reason that thee would be better off there than with thy family."

Thomas turned his eyes her way, his posture rigid. "Had we not made our escape, I might have been able to extract justice for my sister."

The arrogance he carried aboard the boat slipped just enough for Prudence to see a hurt young man wishing vengeance for one he loved more than himself. It was a feeling she could not deny nor lay blame for. She knew it too well.

All she could do was to reach across the space between them to touch the hurting boy's arm. "Father," she prayed, "it is so very easy to ask for vengeance. To seek it ourselves. Please lead the way tonight as three of Thy children find new and safe homes. And, Father, if we might ask, would Thee please ease the minds of those here?" She paused, choosing her words carefully. "And do what Thee will to those whose guilt is known to this family."

Amos offered a hearty, "Amen, Lord," but his grandchildren remained silent.

As they closed the distance to the Ohio shore, Prudence's prayers turned to Thomas and Mary. She prayed for their safety, the success of their futures, but especially to ease the burden and pain of their pasts. All these things she kept quiet, but as the boat butted against the sand, Amos's gaze met hers, and she knew their prayers were the same.

CHAPTER FOURTEEN

An hour or so later LuAnn was unenthusiastically knocking on the door of Apples and Cinnamon. And to think, this used to be one of her favorite rooms. Ellie answered right away, and her first words sent a shockwave through LuAnn.

"I owe you an apology." She flopped down on the bed and affected an exhausted expression. "I have been worrying myself sick over Marsha and have not been sleeping well. I know my expert use of cosmetics covers my dark circles, but they're there. Trust me."

"Okay," LuAnn said. "What specifically are you worrying about in regard to Marsha? Do you think she's in danger?"

"Marsha? *Humph.* Doubtful. She's well able to take care of herself. I'm more worried about her just leaving without a word of goodbye to anyone. I mean, we did have a little fight, but honestly, I can't be expected to take her everywhere, now, can I?"

"I suppose not," LuAnn said.

"Absolutely not." Ellie rolled her eyes. "Imagine trying to go on a date to Boathouse with a chaperone sitting in the back seat. It's just too much."

"I'm sure. So I thought you told me earlier that Marsha was sick. Now you're telling me you're tired because you've known she was missing and have been worried about her." LuAnn paused. "Which is it?"

"Both, of course," she said without missing a beat. "I've been worried about her feeling bad. And now to find out she's gone?"

"And you don't know when she left or how?"

Ellie's brows gathered. "No."

"Or when?"

"No."

"Okay, well then let's talk about the wedding. And when we're done we're going to the police station to tell Officer Goggan what you know."

"Sounds more like we're going to tell him what I don't know," Ellie said.

"You may know something and don't realize it. The officer will want her contact information as well as any other family members she may have reached out to. And for my own peace of mind, since I'm a co-owner of the inn where she was last seen, I would like that same information for our files."

Ellie nodded. "Sure, yeah. Of course. So about the wedding. What are they thinking for the reception tablecloths? Because I had a great idea."

Just like that, the topic moved from missing relatives to wedding planning. LuAnn allowed the change but made a mental note that she would follow up with contact information for Marsha as soon as she could work that question into the conversation.

Unfortunately, Ellie's phone rang, and she announced she simply must go speak to Officer Goggan. "I do so hope he can find Marsha quickly. He was such a dear," she said as she breezed out and left LuAnn sitting in an empty room, wondering how Ellie had managed to make such a quick exit.

"Such a dear?" LuAnn rose, shaking her head. "Oh, brother."

She returned her notebook to her desk upstairs and noticed that Huck hadn't greeted her when she stepped inside the common area. "Huck," she called. "Where are you?"

A whimpering sound came from somewhere in the back of the apartments. She called him again and followed the sound to see that he had somehow ended up behind a closed door in Janice's bedroom.

"Hey there, little guy." LuAnn knelt down to scoop up the ecstatic pup, who promptly offered to share his joy at their reunion with doggie kisses. When she put him down, he ran straight for the door. "You do not need to walk," she told him, but the dog insisted he wanted to be let out.

"I am ignoring you," she told him, then went into her sitting room. Huck followed and made circles around the desk chair until she finally tired of his game. Meanwhile, Tom had relocated to the chair by the window, presumably to watch the show.

"All right," LuAnn said as she straightened a stack of papers that was askew. Turning to the cat, she narrowed her eyes. "Have you been climbing on my desk again?"

In typical Tom fashion, the cat rolled over on his back and stretched, ignoring her. She walked over to the window to scratch his chin, and then paused to enjoy the view one more time.

"You're too good to me, Lord," she whispered as she watched a boat sail past under blue skies on the sparkling water of the Ohio River. "I am humbled by how good You are."

Huck whimpered again. "All right," she told him. She closed the curtains and headed toward the door. "Walking it is."

The next morning, LuAnn opened those same curtains to reveal a far less beautiful scene. Dark clouds had gathered, portending spring rains. Downstairs a few hours later, she was pouring coffee for the lunch crowd when Beverly stepped inside with an umbrella tucked under her arm.

"Good morning," LuAnn called. "It's so good to see you."

Beverly grinned. "I'm meeting my daughter for lunch. Apparently she's got a surprise for me." She leaned in. "I sure hope it's another grandbaby. Wouldn't that just be the best news?"

"It would," LuAnn agreed as Laura stepped inside.

"Why do I get the impression you two are plotting against me?" she said with a grin.

"Not at all, sweetheart." Beverly gave her daughter a hug. "Well, maybe a little. Let's go sit down. I'm eager to find out what this surprise is."

"Before you get too involved in your meal, let's set a time to meet and go over everything for the wedding, shall we?" LuAnn requested.

Laura grinned. "I'm so excited. We've got the church reserved, and Paige is going to sing Mom and Dad's favorite song from their first wedding. The church is already so beautiful, so we were thinking minimal decoration there."

"Minimal decoration is the key to a wedding planner's heart," LuAnn said happily. "So how about we set a day and time to meet and get the rest of this all arranged? I'll see that Ellie is with us when we sit down so she can be up-to-date on everything."

"Sounds perfect," Beverly said. "But again, please, nothing fancy. I am marrying that man because I love him and not because I want a big wedding."

"We know, Mom," Laura said, "but humor me, all right? I did miss the first one, you know."

The women all laughed and then made the arrangements to meet. Then LuAnn went to join Tess in the kitchen as Taylor arrived to take Laura and Beverly to their seats and offer them a menu.

"I love a happy ending," LuAnn said.

"Me too," Tess agreed. "Would you have thought that the man we knew as Camo Dude when we were renovating this place would turn out to be the man that Thorn has become?"

"I know. And now he's marrying Beverly again." LuAnn grinned. "Theoretically, I'm not the real planner of this wedding, but I am just a little bit glad that I have had so much input. I'm really enjoying it."

Robin came through the kitchen with some orders for Winnie. "LuAnn, did I hear you say you're enjoying planning the Thorntons' wedding?"

"You did."

"And aren't you supposed to be helping Ellie Miller?"

"I am. Why?"

"Because when I went up to service Ellie's room just now, it was empty."

"Empty?" Tess said. "What do you mean?"

"I mean cleaned out. As in everything that woman had in there is gone. Did she check out?"

LuAnn and Tess exchanged looks. "No," Tess said. "But wait a second." She went out the kitchen door into the café and came back a minute later. "I asked Janice, and she said she didn't check Ellie out either. She also said she and Winnie would clean up the kitchen so we can deal with this."

"I can also help clean," said Robin.

"We have just under an hour until the café closes," Tess said. "We can go up then and check it out."

When the last customer was chowing down on the last slice of pie, LuAnn and Tess threw off their aprons and raced upstairs. LuAnn got there first and opened the door to find exactly what Robin had told her to expect. As her eyes scanned the room, she found not a shred of evidence that Ellie Miller had ever spent a single night in Apples and Cinnamon.

Tess halted beside her and let out a long breath. "Well now," she said. "I didn't expect this. Did you?"

"No, but maybe she just moved her things into the house she rented from Justin. Do you have a phone number for her?"

"Sure. I think it's the same one we had for Marsha. If I remember correctly, Ellie left her number for both rooms."

She shrugged. "There's only one way to find out. Come downstairs and I'll get it off of her check-in paperwork."

Once they were in the office and Tess found the number, LuAnn placed the call. There was no answer and no voice mail picked up.

She punched in the number for Grant. "Hey there," she said when he answered, keeping her tone light. "I've been trying to call Ellie and can't reach her. I wonder if you might know whether she has moved into that house she leased from Justin."

"I don't know if she's moved in yet, but I do know the signed lease was returned, and she only needed to pick up the keys," he told her. "I can find out if you need me to."

LuAnn met Tess's gaze. "Would you mind terribly?"

"Consider it done."

"Thanks, Grant." LuAnn hung up and turned to Tess. "Now what?"

Janice stepped into the office. "What did I miss?"

"I just spoke to Grant. He's going to find out if Ellie has moved into Justin's rental house yet," LuAnn said. "Her room has been cleared out."

"That's strange." Janice leaned against the doorframe. "So she just left without paying? Or did she leave a credit card on file to take care of the rooms?"

"She did," Tess said. "Or rather Marsha did."

"Marsha?" LuAnn asked.

"Yes, her card has been paying for both rooms since they checked in. She's still paying for both Apples and Cinnamon and Moonlight and Snowflake."

"How?" Janice asked. "Surely she's not calling in."

"No, she left instructions to make daily payments until they check out. So far neither of them have checked out."

"Then maybe they're both planning on coming back," Janice said.

"Doesn't matter to me," Tess said. "As long as the rooms are paid for, that is."

"I guess you're right. It's not up to us to police our guests. If Ellie wants to pursue trying to find Marsha, then that's up to her." LuAnn shrugged. "So we'll continue to keep those rooms reserved for them until they tell us otherwise."

"Or the payments stop," Tess added.

LuAnn grinned. "Now that we have that settled, I'm feeling better about the disappearance of our mystery women."

Then it hit her. Ellie was gone. The wedding planner had left the building.

She turned around to face her friends, but words eluded her.

"What is it?" Janice demanded. "Is something wrong?"

LuAnn shook her head. "I don't know for sure, but I'm about to find out."

She raced upstairs to get her purse and car keys. When she arrived back at the door, Tess and Janice were waiting for her.

"What are you doing?" she asked them.

"Coming with you," Janice said. "I've put Robin in charge, so let's go."

LuAnn shifted her purse onto her shoulder and palmed her keys. "You don't know where I'm going."

"Doesn't matter," Janice said. "The Inn Crowd sticks together."

They piled into LuAnn's car and took off toward the area of town where Ellie's rental was located. "Okay," LuAnn said once they arrived on Cherry Street, "does anyone know which of these houses belongs to Justin O'Hara?"

"It should be easy to tell, shouldn't it?" Janice said.

"Oh, sure. Just look for the one with the fire truck parked in front," Tess said with a snort.

Janice began to laugh, and the other two joined her. They made two trips up and down the street and realized they had no idea which house was the right one.

Finally LuAnn pulled over and parked, then swiveled to look at her friends. "Well, that was a bust," she said. "What's our next move?"

"We could go get the address from Grimes Realty," Janice offered. "Weren't they the ones who listed it?"

"Or I could just call Grant," LuAnn said as she retrieved her phone and tapped on his number.

"Can't talk right now, LuAnn," he said when he picked up the phone. "Dealing with something. Unless it's an emergency."

"No emergency," she said. "Just call me back when you can."

"Will do."

Then he was gone.

Her friends looked at her expectantly.

"Grant was having an emergency. He said he would call when he could."

"Okay, what about Brad?" Tess offered. "He's the other half of Grimes Realty. Even if he isn't the leasing agent, he should have access to the contract. Or at least the address."

"It's worth a try," Janice said.

LuAnn nodded, punched in Brad's number, then sat back to wait for him to answer.

Instead, his voice mail picked up. "This is Brad Grimes. Your call is important, so I'm sorry I missed it. Please leave a message."

"Brad, this is LuAnn. Would you give me a call when you get a chance? Thanks." She hung up and then dialed the real estate office, where she got the same result. "Okay ladies, it looks like we've run out of options."

"No we haven't," Tess said with a grin. "There's always the firehouse. Someone's got to know where Justin's house is. Maybe he'll be on the shift and can tell us himself."

"No way," LuAnn said. "I am not going into the firehouse looking to question Justin O'Hara." She tossed her phone back into her purse, then shifted into Drive. "I'll wait until one of the Grimes brothers calls me back. How long could it take?"

Brad called the next morning just as the breakfast shift was over. "I'm sorry I wasn't able to call back immediately," he told LuAnn. "I've been having trouble with my cell phone and didn't get that message at all. I just now heard the message you left at the office. So how can I help you?"

She took off her apron. "I understand. I wondered if you might be able to tell me the address of Justin's rental."

"Why?" he asked with a wary tone in his voice. "It's already rented."

"Yes," she said. "By Ellie. She cleared out her room here but didn't check out, and she isn't answering her phone. I thought paying her a visit would be the best way of solving the problem."

"Sure. Got a pen?"

"Always," LuAnn said with a smile as she picked up her pen and a napkin. "Whenever you're ready."

He gave her the address. "I hope this helps. Seems odd that she would forget to check out though."

"This is Ellie we're talking about," LuAnn said. "Thanks for the help."

"Anytime," he told her.

She hung up, then went upstairs and grabbed her purse, keys, and sleuthing notebook. She found Janice and Tess deep in conversation in the kitchen. "I've got the address," she said, waving the notebook.

"Great," Janice said. "Let's go."

"You two go ahead," Tess said. "Someone's got to mind the store."

"Are you sure you don't mind?" Janice said.

"Go on." Tess shooed them out. "I've got plenty to do. But I want all the details when you get back."

"We promise," LuAnn said, then hurried outside. She climbed into the car and handed the notebook to Janice. They made the short drive to Cherry Street, where LuAnn slowed her car down so Janice could read the numbers on the houses.

"There," she said as she pointed up ahead to a small brick house wedged between two other houses of slightly grander size. "There's no car in the driveway. What should we do?"

LuAnn shrugged as she parked the car and turned off the engine. "We pay her a visit."

They made their way to the front door and knocked. No response. LuAnn searched for a doorbell but found none. After glancing around to be sure they weren't being observed, she leaned up on tiptoe and peered inside. The kitchen was spare but tidy. Nothing cluttered up the room that she could see, and there were no dishes in the sink.

She turned around to see that Janice had disappeared. It only took a moment to realize her friend had made her way into the backyard. LuAnn found her standing on a small brick patio, her hands resting on her hips. "What did you find?" LuAnn asked.

"Nothing," Janice said. "The curtains are shut tight, and it's too cold for anyone to have lawn furniture out, so the empty patio proves nothing."

"All right," LuAnn said. "All we can do is leave a note on the door and hope she sees it."

Once that was accomplished, the women drove back to the inn and reported to Tess.

"So we don't know anything more than we did before?" she asked them.

"Other than the address, no," LuAnn said.

"Then we just hope she sees the note," Tess stated. "And in the meantime, we keep sleuthing and keep letting Marsha pay for two rooms that no one is using."

"I suppose you're right." LuAnn tucked her keys into her purse and stowed it in the back of the office, and then turned to face her friends. "But we're going to solve the mystery of where these ladies disappeared to, even if they are paying their bills, right?"

"Definitely," Tess said as Janice nodded in agreement.

The next day, Friday, had all hands on deck. Hunting down Ellie and wedding planning had taken a back seat to another, more pressing matter, namely, preparing the inn for a weekend of stargazing by the local astronomy club.

The event had been on the books since well before Christmas and included two nights of telescope time at the Anderson Hancock Planetarium, an afternoon of digging for meteorites in a special area of the New Concord meteorite strewn field, and a Gazing with the Stars gala where the winner of the annual Astronomer of the Year would be announced.

Winnie had declared that the café would be closed tomorrow and had been baking star-shaped cookies all afternoon in anticipation of the several dozen attendees who would converge on them this evening for an after-gazing gathering on this opening day of the event. LuAnn sat at the table with her notebook, the warm scent of chocolate swirling around her from the brownies that had just come from the oven.

"Turning regular brownies into meteorite brownies was a stroke of genius," LuAnn said as she tasted a tiny piece of one. "The chopped nuts you added are perfect. Delicious."

"I think they'll like them," Winnie said. "But I'm only serving decaf coffee tonight. I never thought I would get those folks out of here last night. Goodness knows I'm not as young as I used to be, so I sure don't plan on having them here until all hours. But I'm truly thankful for the overtime. My old car's been making more noises than my knees."

LuAnn chuckled. "They were very enthusiastic, weren't they? So enthusiastic they started their weekend early with that little get-together last night. It's a good thing you make a habit of keeping treats in the freezer, Winnie. Who knew astronomers were so much fun?"

"You call it what you want, but I don't think it sounds like fun to stare up into space for a living." She shook her head. "Give me a job where I can stir a pot or bake a loaf of bread and get paid for it, and I am a happy woman."

LuAnn walked over to hug Winnie. "You make the three of us happy women, my friend. Thank you for all the hard work you do. I don't know that we tell you enough how very much we appreciate you."

"I do love what I do here," she said with a grin.

A roar went up outside, alerting LuAnn that the astronomers were arriving. "I'd better go see if they need anything," she said.

"You go ahead," Winnie told her. "I'm going to stand right here and thank the good Lord that they're a local club and all go home to their own beds. Can you imagine the noise if they were all staying here?"

As LuAnn turned to head toward the door, her phone rang, and she reached for it.

"Sorry it took so long for me to return your call," Grant said. "I got your message and can text over the address if you still need it."

"No problem. Brad already gave it to me. So, I hope the emergency wasn't too awful."

"Actually, it was pretty awful. There was a break-in at my house."

"Oh no. That's terrible."

"It could have been worse," he said. "I wasn't home when it happened."

"Did they take much?"

"Not really." He paused. "That's what's so strange. They tried to get into my safe but weren't successful. A few things were thrown around and broken, but nothing that I'll lose any sleep over."

"That's a relief."

"Yes. Except they did take my negatives."

"Which ones?" she asked.

"All of them."

"Oh, Grant. No." She gripped the phone, aware than Winnie was now staring at her. "But that's all of your art, right? Your photographs weren't digital."

"That's right," he said with a chuckle that held no humor. "So all the people who got prints from me now have collector's items."

Later that night when the last of the stargazers had gone home, LuAnn climbed into bed and rested her head on her pillow to pray, adding a special request for Grant's lost negatives to be found. When she opened her eyes she glanced over at the table where her Grant Grimes collector's item photograph was.

Or should have been.

It was gone.

CHAPTER FIFTEEN

"The last time I remember the picture being there was Tuesday night," LuAnn said the next morning as she sat on the edge of her bed and wiped her eyes with the already damp tissue. "It could have disappeared any time after that. It was the eight-by-ten Grant gave me of his photo of the couple at the park across the street. I've never moved it except to dust, because it's special to me."

She burst into tears again, not yet able to explain to her best friends the depth of her loss. Seeing the empty place where she'd hidden the most important things in the world to her was like losing her father all over again.

Huck alternated between nudging her elbow and climbing in and out of her lap. Tom huddled close next to her and purred.

Janice reached over to offer her another tissue. "I'm so sorry," she said. "I wish I knew how to make this better. I want to fix it for you."

LuAnn shook her head. "It can't be fixed," she said. "What I lost can't be replaced."

"Because Grant's negatives were stolen?" Tess asked.

LuAnn dried her eyes and straightened her back, then allowed her gaze to shift from Tess to Janice and back to Tess again. "Because what was hidden behind that photograph is something I can never replace."

Tess wrapped a protective arm around her. "What was behind the photograph?" she asked gently.

Letting out a long breath, LuAnn gripped the tissue in her fist. "A letter from my father and the only picture I have of us together."

"Oh honey," Tess said. "I'm so very sorry."

"Oh no." Janice touched her arm. "No wonder you're distraught."

"I know." LuAnn shrugged. "It's so stupid. I should have put them away for safekeeping or scanned them, but I liked the idea that they were there on my nightstand, just for me to know they were there and not to show everyone. Isn't that silly? It sounds that way when I say it. But I just wanted that last part of my dad to be for me only."

"No," Tess said. "It's not silly if it's how you feel."

"Absolutely not," Janice said. "We're all so different, and how we handle our grief is as different as we are. I cannot tell you how many women I counseled over the years, and no two of them reacted in the same way to the death of the ones they loved. One lady I specifically recall wanted every picture of her husband taken off the wall in her home but kept them all in a box by her bed. She felt comforted that he was nearby but wasn't hit with fresh grief every time she saw an image of him."

"That's it exactly," LuAnn said, almost managing a smile as she ran her hand down Huck's back and then Tom's. "It was such a comfort to know if I wanted to see his photo or read his letter, all I had to do was pick the picture up and look behind it…"

And there were the tears again. She gave in and allowed Tess and Janice to comfort her. Finally, when she thought she had no more tears left, she let her friends convince her to come into the sitting area for a cup of tea. Ever her shadow, Huck trotted a step behind while Tom took advantage of the empty nightstand to curl up in the spot where the photograph had once rested.

"All right, ladies," Tess said in her most authoritative voice. "I think we realize that we cannot sit idly by without doing something. What has happened right here under our roof is completely unacceptable. We've got to find LuAnn's photograph."

"Which may have disappeared the same time as Ellie," LuAnn said. "Do you think the two are linked?"

"Has she ever been up here?" Janice asked.

"Just to meet with me about the wedding," LuAnn said. "But I was with her the whole time. She picked up the picture and talked about how much she liked it, then she put it down again. You know, as long as we're talking about missing items, Grant's theft happened around the same time, didn't it?"

"Yes, all of this is suspicious," Tess said. "But right now we need to call the police and let them know we've had something stolen from the inn."

"But it's nothing of great value to anyone but me," LuAnn protested. "Do you think they would even bother?"

"Of course they will," Tess said. "You forget I have a friend at the station. I'll call Chief Mayfield and let him know something precious has been taken from my best friend, and we'd like someone to investigate. Keep in mind, whoever took that photograph was walking around right here in our apartments."

Janice shuddered. "That's a terrible thought. I wonder if we should look around and make certain that nothing else was taken."

"Yes," Tess said. "I think that's an excellent idea. It's much better to have a full inventory of any losses we've suffered before we call. And actually, I think we need to make sure that nothing was taken from other places in the inn. I'll ask Robin to look around to see if we're missing anything in the guest rooms. Winnie probably ought to do an audit of the kitchen."

"You know what's funny—only not funny?" Janice said. "My first thought when you said we should see what's missing from the inn is that we already know Ellie and Marsha are missing. Do you think this theft could be connected to Ellie just up and running off during the night?"

"I do." Tess shook her head. "And while I'm thinking of it, how in the world could that woman leave during the night without one of us hearing the buzzer that sounds up here every time a door is opened downstairs?"

"Oh," LuAnn said, "that's a very good question. I didn't hear anything the night before we discovered she was gone. Did either of you?"

"Not a thing," Janice said.

"What did she do, climb out the window?" LuAnn said. "With all of those suitcases, I can't see how that would be possible. Or why she would want to do that." She frowned. "None of this makes sense."

The buzzer sounded, alerting them to a door opening down on the first floor.

"See," Tess said. "We would have heard that the night she disappeared."

LuAnn shook her head. "Just thinking about all of this makes my head hurt. The first thing I'm going to do is get some breakfast. Then I'm going to take Tess's suggestion and go inventory my sitting room and bedroom, and I suggest you two do the same. Does anyone see anything missing in here?"

"Nope," Tess said after her gaze swept the room.

"Me neither," Janice agreed.

"Divide and conquer then," LuAnn said. "After breakfast we inventory our apartments, and then we muster the troops downstairs to see if anything else is missing."

After a quick bowl of cereal, LuAnn searched her bedroom and found nothing else missing, not even from her jewelry box. Then she went into the sitting room to take a closer look. Everything seemed in order, so she moved to her desk and sat down.

Nothing appeared to have been moved since she'd straightened things after Tom rearranged her desktop. One by one, she pulled open the drawers to check the contents.

And it wasn't there.

"Tess, Janice!" she called.

"What did you find?" Janice hurried into the sitting room with Tess a step behind.

LuAnn gestured to her desk drawer. "My camera is gone."

Tess shook her head. "Interesting coincidence, that the wedding planner and picture and the camera disappear at the same time."

"It is interesting," Janice said. "If there's nothing else missing up here, let's go downstairs and talk to Robin and Winnie."

They found the two women in the kitchen. Robin was turning pages of Winnie's cookbook while Winnie looked on. Both glanced up as LuAnn stepped inside.

"What's wrong?" Winnie demanded.

"We've had a theft," LuAnn told her. "Some things were stolen from my apartment. We're going to need to do an inventory of the building to see if anything else is missing."

After a thorough search of the inn, the ladies all met back in the kitchen to determine that the only losses had been in LuAnn's rooms. Tess called Chief Mayfield to give him the news and ask his advice.

"Alaskan cruise?" Tess said. "That sounds wonderful." She paused. "No, don't you worry about it. Have a great trip."

"Unfortunately, the chief and his wife are on an Alaskan cruise. He was just about to shut his phone down in Seattle to board the ship when I called."

"Oh, that's too bad," Janice said. "Well, good for the Mayfields, but bad for us."

"He's sending poor Officer Goggan back," she said. "Apparently he's got the most background on what could become a series of related cases."

"Related cases?" LuAnn asked. "Does he mean our two guests disappearing and then my photograph and the camera going missing too? He's thinking the same thing we are?"

"He didn't say." Tess shrugged. "I guess we'll have to wait for Officer Goggan to fill us in."

The familiar policeman arrived shortly afterward. Before he delved into the new facts the ladies had discovered, he walked straight into the kitchen and gave Winnie a hug.

"That's from my mother," he told her. "She was feeling under the weather, and that soup you sent me home with perked her right up. She told me to tell you if you don't have a name for it, you should call that concoction Winnie Washington's Medicinal Soup. It made her day."

Winnie laughed. "You tell your mama that her kind words have made *my* day."

"I will do that, ma'am." He sobered. "All right, ladies, it seems like we've been making a habit of this." He nodded toward the table, and they all sat down. "Chief Mayfield has filled me in on the missing items, but I'd like to hear from you what happened." He nodded to LuAnn. "Miss Sherrill, why don't you start?"

"Robin discovered Ellie's empty room, which concerned us since we never heard anyone leave and she didn't check out."

"You thought she skipped out?" the officer asked.

"No, the rooms are being paid for by credit card daily."

He nodded. "And you had a big group here last night, am I right?"

"We did," she said. "The local astronomers had their gala."

"How many attended?"

Tess spoke up. "They made arrangements for forty. I haven't checked yet, but I believe that's how many they had."

"All right, can you get ahold of whoever booked the event and ask for a guest list? Then I'll need to follow up on anyone else who might have been in the inn from the time the cousin went missing until this morning."

Tess gasped. "That's going to be a long list."

"Yes," Janice said. "Between the astronomers last night, and our café customers, there could be any number of people."

Officer Goggan shrugged. "It may seem like that's the case, but you'd be surprised how fast some of these folks can be ruled out. If you all will work on your list, that would be a great help."

"Of course," Tess said as LuAnn and Janice nodded.

He turned to LuAnn. "Do you have anything to add to what has already been said?"

"Just one thing," she said. "That picture that's missing from my room is the same one that Ellie Miller purchased from Grant at First Friday. Why would she want to steal something she already owned?"

"You're certain it's the same one?" he asked.

"I'm positive."

The officer nodded and scribbled another note on his pad. LuAnn smiled despite the occasion. It was always nice to meet another list maker.

"And you, Winnie," he said as he swiveled toward her. "You're the only one I haven't heard from."

"Oh, please," she told him. "Once I get started on that woman, I may not stop. And not a word of what would come out of my mouth would be based on anything but speculation and years of experience with people like her. Nor would it be edifying speech, and ever since two Sundays ago when I got convicted about the words of my mouth, I have tried not to say what I ought not to say."

He suppressed a grin. "All right, then, I will just assume that you do not hold Miss Miller in high regard, and you believe she's behind the thefts and her cousin's disappearance."

Winnie nodded. "I think she stole Grant Grimes's negatives too, or knows who did."

"I'm glad you brought that up," he said. "Do any of you know anything about that theft?"

"Only what Grant told me," LuAnn said. "And that was just that it happened. No details other than he said he lost all his negatives."

"He was with that Ellie Miller, wasn't he?" Winnie said.

The police officer swung his attention to Winnie. "He was, actually."

She nodded. "I knew it. See, I told you ladies that she wasn't what she said she was, and I sure didn't think she and that supposed cousin of hers were anything but actors pretending."

"She did say that," Janice acknowledged.

"And I knew from the beginning," Tess said. "Something about that pair just didn't add up."

"There's a lot here that doesn't add up," LuAnn said. "What do you make of it, Officer Goggan?"

He shrugged. "I'm trying to keep an open mind. What we have here are two incidents where photographs were stolen in one form or another. So there could be something that ties them together, but I haven't figured out what that is."

"I bet she's got a boyfriend out there somewhere," Winnie said. "Because I don't think for a minute that a woman like her would be partners in crime with another female, cousin or not. I think that Marsha character—or whoever she is—is not responsible for anything other than having the bad luck to know Ellie Miller." She paused. "Or whoever she is."

"Okay," LuAnn said. "I don't know about the boyfriend angle, but Brad and I met her brother the other day."

"Her brother?" Tess's eyes were like saucers. "You never mentioned she had a brother."

"I didn't think of it," LuAnn said with a shrug. "He was passing through town and stopped to see her. Brad and I were leaving the Sassy Seamstress and saw the two of them talking."

"I bet she didn't like that," Winnie said. "I don't believe he's her brother. Like I said, he's more likely a boyfriend she doesn't want to be seen with."

"She did say Gino was adopted," LuAnn admitted.

"Gino?" the policeman said. "What was his last name?"

"Miller, maybe?" She shrugged. "They didn't say, I just assumed it was."

"I'm going to need a description of him and the car he was driving," he said. "And I will need you and Brad Grimes to come down to the station to talk to our sketch artist. If we can find this guy, maybe we've got an accomplice."

"Do you think he might come back?" Janice asked, her brows furrowed.

"We have no way of knowing," he told her. "Which means you all need to be careful until we get to the bottom of this. Keep your apartment doors locked, and keep the door to every room locked as well."

"We always do," Janice said.

"Well, to the rooms," Tess said. "We don't always remember to lock the doors to our apartments. At least I don't."

"Nor do I," LuAnn admitted. "But we do have Huck up there to alert us to intruders." She paused and shook her head.

"What is it?" Janice asked.

"I found Huck in your room a couple of days ago," LuAnn said. "It was…let me see…Wednesday. I just thought maybe he'd slipped in there behind you and then gotten trapped inside. Now I wonder."

"And I wondered why there was an empty can of tuna in my sitting room," Janice said.

"Huck does love tuna," LuAnn said. "So whoever took my photograph and my camera plied our dog with tuna, and then closed him up in Janice's room so if he barked we wouldn't hear him."

Officer Goggan grinned. "We could use people with your detective skills on the police force."

"No, thank you," LuAnn said. "I like what I'm doing just fine."

"So do we," Janice and Tess said in unison.

"All right. I think I've got what I need to get started. Miss Sherrill, if you'll get together with Mr. Grimes and give your statements and description as soon as possible, that would be great. And if the rest of you could compile the list of names, I'd appreciate that."

"I'll call Brad right now," LuAnn said. "And thank you all so much for your help in finding my photo. These two ladies already know this, but there's more than a picture in that frame. Two items that were precious to me were hidden in the frame behind that photograph. So even though it doesn't seem like I lost much personally, I did."

"Oh, Miss Lu," Winnie said. "I had no idea. We're going to pray that the Lord leads this policeman right to wherever those lost things are hidden."

"Thank you, Winnie." She turned her attention to Officer Goggan. "I wish we could figure out why someone would take that particular photograph. That would make things so much easier."

"Maybe we can," Brad said as he stepped into the kitchen.

Chapter Sixteen

May 4, 1860

The professor climbed out of the boat first, followed by Amos and then Thomas. Prudence waited while Thomas lifted his sister out and set her on dry land. He reached over to offer help to Prudence, and she smiled.

"Thank you, Thomas. You are a great help. I believe the Lord has meant you for great things."

He gave her what might almost have been a hopeful look. He opened his mouth to speak and then seemed to think better of it. Offering a smile, he ducked his head and followed his grandfather and the professor up the path away from the river.

As she watched the young woman picking her way down the path, her heavy skirts trailing her, a thought occurred. Prudence caught up to Professor Ashworth. "Would thee mind stopping briefly at my home?"

"Any delay could bring disaster," he protested. "Why would you want me to bring them there before I take them to the college?"

She nodded toward Mary. "A suitable change of attire," she said. "I have something for her that will not attract so much attention."

He glanced back at Mary, then returned his attention to Prudence. "An excellent idea."

A few minutes later, the lights of the farmhouse came into view. Jason hurried to meet them, first shaking the professor's hand, then gathering Prudence into a tight embrace. "I found the ribbon," he said, "but thee had already gone."

"I did not know the professor was one of us," she said. She rested her cheek against his shoulder. "I could not take the risk."

"I understand," he said before he turned to the three strangers. "Now tell me who I have the honor of meeting."

Introductions were made, and the men fell into conversation over the meager remains of what Jason had found in the kitchen. Prudence took Mary aside.

"Thy gown is lovely," she told her. "But perhaps thee might wish to not stand out so much among the townspeople?"

Mary nodded. Until that moment, Prudence hadn't realized the young woman had not said a word the entire time she'd been in her presence.

"All right, then." Prudence smiled. "It's just in here. We will have to be very quiet. My son is asleep."

Mary followed without question and stood very quietly as Prudence closed the door and tiptoed over to the peg to remove her Sunday dress. It was only partly pressed, as she had never gone back to finish the task that had been interrupted when Jason returned home.

She handed the dress to Mary. "Do you need help?"

Mary shook her head, so Prudence glanced over at her sleeping son, and then left Mary to change her clothes. The men had moved their conversation to the porch, leaving Prudence to wait alone. After a while, when it seemed the young woman had more than enough time to change clothes, Prudence heard Moses's whimpers and knocked.

"Mary, may I come in? It sounds like Moses is awake."

The soft sound of singing was her only response as Prudence slowly swung the door open. She found Mary on the floor beside Moses's cot in Prudence's Sunday dress. Moonlight streamed in through the open windows, framing the girl in silver light.

Moses sat contentedly in her lap worrying with the sleeve of the cotton dress just as he always did during Sunday services. The song continued, a melody that sounded familiar in a language that did not. After a few minutes, Moses climbed from Mary's lap and toddled toward Prudence.

She scooped the little boy into her arms and offered Mary a smile. "Thank you for seeing to Moses."

Mary rose and straightened the wrinkles on the dress. Slowly she turned her attention to Prudence and smiled. Even in the shapeless cotton gown, with a length of fabric for a belt, Mary looked as regal as a princess.

"There is food for thee in the kitchen," Prudence offered. She placed a wiggling Moses back down on the floor.

Mary merely smiled as Prudence led her to the table and set the plate in front of her. She ate in dainty bites, pausing between each one as if to savor each morsel. When the plate was empty, Mary rose and followed the voices out onto the porch.

Prudence stepped out behind the girl and surveyed the men seated on the porch while Moses toddled past. Mary had discovered Patience and was stroking the goose's feathered back.

"Your granddaughter has been fed and is ready to go. I'll just fold up her dress so it will travel better, and you can be on your way."

Mary looked up sharply. "No."

"No?" Prudence shook her head. "To what?"

"The dress," she said. "I don't want it."

"But it's lovely," Prudence protested. "And finely made."

Amos stepped up beside Mary. "She'd be the one to decide. You've given her a fine dress to wear, and we are much obliged. Soon as I can get proper clothes for these two I will send back what she's borrowed."

"No," Prudence said. "It is hers to keep. I would be honored to trade for so lovely a dress." Of course she would never wear such an opulent gown, but cut into pieces it would make a fine quilt.

"I only wish I had something to offer to the men," Jason said. "I fear all I have is on my back."

Amos reached to shake hands with Jason. "You and your wife and this man Ashworth here have given me and my grandchildren more than anyone else ever could. Thanks to you, we are free."

"Free but not yet safe," Professor Ashworth warned. "We've stayed longer than we should. We must leave now else we could risk capture."

Jason nodded and took a step backward. "Go thee with God," he told the older man before turning his attention to Thomas. Before her husband could say anything, Thomas grasped him in a hug that lifted his toes off the ground.

"I'll do what you said," Thomas said when he released him.

"See that thee does," Jason called as he watched the three walk with the professor toward the road that led into Marietta.

When the travelers were out of sight, Prudence nudged her husband. "What did you tell Thomas to do?"

Jason offered a slow smile. "I just challenged him to take his anger and turn it into something that will show those who held him captive that he is their equal."

"How can he do that?"

"He asked the same thing. I told him if they said he was stupid, then he should get an education. If they treated him like he was an animal, then he must stand up and be a good man to others." He shrugged. "And above all, he should look to the Lord for everything, giving thanks first and foremost for any blessing He bestows."

"Good advice," she told him as Moses tugged at her skirt.

"Indeed, I thought so," Jason said. "And my next advice is that it is getting late, and the morning will come early. Shall we find our bed, Wife?"

She tucked Moses up on her shoulder, and the little one immediately stilled. "It appears Moses already has."

Chapter Seventeen

LuAnn scooted over and made room for Brad at the kitchen table. "Do you know something?" She paused. "And how did you know to stop by? I was about to call you."

"One question at a time," he said with a chuckle as he joined them at the table. "I was driving by the inn and saw the police car. I thought I'd better see if you ladies were all right."

Winnie got up and started taking mugs out of the cupboard. "We need some coffee if we're gonna sit here much longer," she mumbled.

Brad looked around the table. "I've been thinking about this ever since Grant's studio was broken into. I couldn't figure out why the thief only took film and negatives when much more expensive things were left alone. It just made no sense." He leaned forward and rested his elbows on the table. "But when you stop looking at what wasn't taken and you look at what was taken, then a pattern emerges."

"I'm glad someone can see one," Janice said, "because it makes no sense to me."

"The photograph Ellie bought from Grant is the same one LuAnn had stolen, and the negatives that were taken from Grant's studio included that image." Brad sat back. "I think whoever is responsible wants to remove any evidence of that particular picture."

"But Ellie owns a print of that photograph," LuAnn said.

"Exactly," Brad said. "You told me she was adamant that she had to have that picture. Well, maybe she had to have every copy of it."

"But why?" LuAnn's eyes widened. "Brad! What if the couple in that photograph is Ellie and someone she doesn't want to be seen with?"

"Like her brother?" he said. "Think hard. Do you remember what the couple looked like in the photograph?"

LuAnn closed her eyes and tried to recall. "They were in profile," she said. "So it's hard to tell. The woman's hair was in a ponytail and maybe was straight. I think it was, anyway. And the man..." She opened her eyes and shook her head. "I just remember broad shoulders, and I think he was sort of muscular. I loved the picture because it reminded me of the view out of my sitting room, not because of the people in it."

"Broad shoulders and muscular," Brad echoed. "Like a certain guy named Gino?"

Winnie waved a mug in triumph. "I told you—she has a boyfriend."

Brad smiled over at Winnie. "She very well could."

Officer Goggan nodded. "What you're saying makes sense. If there's a reason why she didn't want to be seen with her brother"—he looked to Winnie—"or boyfriend, then it would make sense to get rid of the evidence. But why take the camera that was in Miss Sherrill's desk?"

"LuAnn was taking pictures at the First Friday gathering," Tess said. "And Ellie was there. Do you think she doesn't want *any* picture of herself around?"

"She took LuAnn's camera?" Brad accepted a cup of coffee. "Thank you, Winnie. Why wouldn't she want us to see a picture of her?" he asked. "She just put down a deposit and paid rent on Justin's house on Cherry Street. It's not like everybody and their brother hasn't seen her in town."

Officer Goggan scribbled a note in his pad. "Do you know the address on Cherry Street?" he asked Brad.

"I have it." LuAnn retrieved her phone and read the address out loud to the officer.

Officer Goggan put his notebook away. "I think I've got enough to go on. I'll go pay Ellie a visit at her new place, but I still need that description of this Gino character, so I'd appreciate it if you two would do that as soon as possible."

Brad looked over at LuAnn. "Are you busy right now?"

"No," she said.

He returned his attention to the policeman. "Sounds like we're about to go give your sketch artist a description."

"Tess and I will work on that list of who's been here," Janice piped in. "Maybe that'll be of some help."

"Thank you all," he said as he walked out with Brad and LuAnn. He paused at the door of his squad car and looked at the two of them. "I know I haven't been on the force that long, but I can't remember any case like this one. I get someone wanting to cover up a meeting that accidentally got caught on film, but what's her motive for that? I mean, who cares if she was hanging out with some guy at the park?"

Brad and LuAnn discussed that question on the way to the police station.

"I think they were partners in crime," Brad said.

"Think or believe?" LuAnn asked.

He hesitated. "Think," he finally said.

"Well, I'm more inclined to believe Winnie's right. This guy was a boyfriend. Maybe Ellie's family disapproved of him."

His brows rose. "They don't strike me as the Romeo and Juliet type."

"Fair enough. But what about Marsha?" LuAnn said. "Where does she fit in all of this? She just packed up and left sometime on Saturday morning—at least that's what Ellie says, and has never come back."

"And you said Ellie alternated between being unconcerned and distraught?"

"She did, but I'm telling you, there wasn't a single time I saw them together that they actually looked like they enjoyed being in one another's company. That just seems odd if they are actually related."

He signaled to turn into the parking lot adjacent to police headquarters and shrugged. "I feel that way about Grant sometimes, so it doesn't seem out of the ordinary to me that family would be at odds on occasion."

"I suppose that could be true, especially if Ellie had a boyfriend Marsha didn't like."

"Or they weren't family at all," Brad suggested as he pulled into a parking space.

"Now we're just talking in circles," LuAnn said. "Are they family or not? Is the mystery man a boyfriend or a brother or an accomplice? It all just refuses to gel into a single theory that works."

"I agree." Brad got out and went around to open LuAnn's door. "Which is why we are not detectives."

"That's true," LuAnn said, "although the Inn Crowd has solved a mystery or two."

Brad grinned, and the effect was dazzling. She shared his smile and congratulated herself for her still heart. Just because Brad Grimes had those dimples and that lovely set of blue eyes, that didn't mean she had any feelings for him other than friendship.

And for now, that was just the way she liked it.

After they finished meeting with the sketch artist, they stepped outside. "Why don't we take a drive down Cherry Street? Not to get in the middle of an investigation," he assured her, "but just to say hello to the new tenant."

"And see if she needs any help unpacking?" LuAnn offered. "I'm kidding," she said when she saw his expression.

Brad signaled to turn onto Cherry Street and immediately hit the brakes, pulled over, and turned off the car. Three police cars, all with lights flashing, were stopped in front of the rental. Two blocked the road while one sat parallel to the curb in front. There were no vehicles in the driveway of any kind.

"Wow," LuAnn said as Brad nodded in agreement. "What do you think they found?"

"I don't see the SWAT team," he quipped. "So my guess is they're just searching the property. Officer Goggan wouldn't have done that alone, so they probably have some sort of protocol for having multiple officers at a scene."

"I suppose." She paused. "I hope they haven't found Marsha, if you know what I mean."

"Hey, check out what's coming up beside us." Brad pointed at the rearview mirror. "They sure are in a hurry."

LuAnn turned in her seat in time to see two black Suburbans with tinted windows race past at high speed. They darted around the roadblock set up by the police cars and pulled into the driveway of the little rental house.

"Maybe they've found Marsha," LuAnn said. "Or something worse."

Brad let out a long breath. "Yeah, well, I don't know what to do right now. I mean, we are technically the leasing agents, and Grant did tell me he left a For Rent sign in the garage that he needed to pick up sometime this week." He shrugged. "But I don't think now is the time to do that."

"Me neither," she said as multiple people in dark clothing bounded out of the Suburbans and disappeared inside the garage.

Brad glanced over at her. "You know those weren't regular cops, right? They don't show up in dark Suburbans." He paused. "There's only one group of folks who arrive like that."

"Men in Black?" she quipped.

He shook his head but allowed a grin. "Feds, LuAnn. That's FBI, CIA, Homeland Security, or some other agency with initials, or possibly some combination of all of the above. What that is not, is local law enforcement."

"Wow," she said again, her gaze trained on the two SUVs. "This is bigger than we thought, Brad."

"I would say so." He shrugged, then drummed his fingers on the steering wheel. "So now what?"

She turned to look at him. "We go back to the inn and let the others know."

As it turned out, the others were well aware. Two Suburbans matching the ones LuAnn and Brad had just left on Cherry Street were parked at the inn's front entrance. In contrast to the scene at Ellie's rental, there were no police cars visible.

Brad parked across the street and got out to help LuAnn from the car. As she climbed out, Paige walked swiftly past.

"Hi, Paige," LuAnn called. "No baby yet?"

"Not yet, but the doctor said to keep walking," she said as she picked up her pace. "So I keep walking."

"So I see." LuAnn smiled at her and nodded toward the inn. "If you ever get tired of walking, stop in for a cup of tea. Decaf, of course. Or fruit juice. Or water. Or whatever you like."

"Thank you, LuAnn. I will," she said with a wave as she turned the corner and disappeared from sight.

"I'm convinced that woman is going to jog all the way to the hospital," Brad said with a chuckle.

"She might," LuAnn agreed. He opened the door for her, and she stepped inside.

The café was empty, and none of the seats in the lobby were occupied.

Grant met them at the door. "Why didn't you answer your phone?" he demanded of Brad.

"It never rang," he said as he reached into his pocket. "Oh, it was on silent. Looks like I've got three missed calls and a whole bunch of texts." He looked back up at Grant. "All from you, I guess?"

"I didn't count, but probably," Grant said. "Could I speak with you privately?"

LuAnn gave them a smile. "I'm just going to go find Janice and Tess."

"Tess is in the office, and Janice is in the kitchen," Grant said before he stepped toward the café with Brad. "But you can't go either place," he said over his shoulder.

"Just watch me." LuAnn headed for the office and found the door blocked by a burly man in a black suit. "Tess?" she called. She pressed past the man to find her friend seated at her desk. "What's going on?"

Tess smiled up at LuAnn and nodded to the man seated across from her. With his military-style haircut and athletic frame, he looked familiar. "You remember Agent Charles Butler of the FBI, don't you, LuAnn?"

He swiveled around to smile at LuAnn, and then nodded at the hulk of a man who was crowding in behind her. "She's fine," he said. "Why don't you watch the front door?"

LuAnn nodded. "Yes, of course I do." She shook his hand, then took the seat next to him. "As I recall, you have twins. How are they? And how have you been?"

"All is well," he told her. "Thank you for asking." His expression sobered. "However, as you have probably guessed, this is not a social visit."

"This is about Ellie," she supplied. "And Marsha?"

"Yes, that's right." He paused. "Tess has been catching me up on what happened here the past few days. I wish I could say I'm surprised, but unfortunately, I'm not."

Tess looked at LuAnn, and then back at Agent Butler. "Do you want to tell her, or should I?"

He shook his head. "I will," he said, followed by a sigh. "I knew when I saw this place last year that it was a nice inn in a quiet community, and that you ladies were honest, trustworthy, and just plain good people."

"Well, thank you," LuAnn said. "But why do I feel like there's more to that?"

"There's a lot more, but I can't tell you much of it. Suffice it to say that when we need a place for someone to stay where we can keep them safe and out of the public eye, we look to quiet places like this with innkeepers or owners like you."

Her eyes narrowed. "You're talking about the witness protection program, aren't you?"

He gave her a curt nod. "We refer to it as the Witness Security Program or WITSEC, but yes."

Tess gave her an empathetic look. "I know," she said to LuAnn.

The agent's attention went from Tess to LuAnn. "Am I missing something?"

"LuAnn's father disappeared when she was a child," Tess said. "Not so long ago she found out why."

"WITSEC?" he asked LuAnn, and she managed to nod. "I'm so sorry. I can't imagine how difficult that was. There's nothing I can say to help ease your pain over that loss, but as an agent I can tell you that I have nothing but the deepest respect for a man who would give up everything he held dear in order to do the right thing and give testimony that will put a perpetrator away."

Tears gathered, but she blinked them back. In all the time since she'd known what happened to her father, she had never heard from anyone on the other side of the program. From someone who understood the sacrifice her father had made.

"Thank you," she managed. "That does help."

"We at the Bureau are very aware that those under our protection are giving up more than they ever thought they would. Sometimes we pair those folks with someone who can help them make the transition. During the time before they testify, however, they are usually escorted by a United States Marshal."

LuAnn met Tess's even gaze. "Are we talking about Ellie and Marsha?" At her nod, LuAnn continued. "And are we being told which is which?"

"Under normal circumstances I wouldn't even be here," he said. "However, for a couple of reasons—namely, that I trust you but also that I feel you ought to know enough to be able to navigate any future situations—I am going to tell you more than I typically would." Agent Butler paused. "However, I need you to promise me that what I tell you won't go any further than the three of us."

"We need to make that the four of us," LuAnn said. "Janice should be included in this."

"Yes, of course," he said. "I believe she's in the kitchen with one of my associates. I seem to remember you ladies having apartments up on the top floor. Why don't we get her and move up there?"

A few minutes later, all four of them plus a burly man who stood on the other side of the door were relocated to the women's common room at the top of the inn. Agent Butler notified Brad and Grant of the meeting but did not invite them to participate. The agents stood in the hallway, and Tess had just caught Janice up on everything they had learned thus far.

"Winnie has just taken an apple pie out of the oven," Janice said. "I doubt the Grimes brothers will miss us for a while."

"Yes, but they're going to want an explanation," LuAnn said as she scratched Huck behind the ears.

"I'm afraid you won't be able to tell them anything."

CHAPTER EIGHTEEN

Agent Butler seated himself in the empty chair, and Tom jumped in his lap to peer up at him. In response, the agent scratched under the cat's chin. "Here is what I can tell you. Yes, Ellie and Marsha are participating in WITSEC. No, I cannot tell you which is which. The idea of bringing them here was mine, and for all the reasons I have already stated, I believe it was a good one." He paused. "What you don't realize is, I've already done this once before."

"You're kidding," Janice said.

"Oh, who was it?" Tess asked.

"I can't say. But as long as I feel my people are safe here, I will continue to consider this a good spot to offer up when it fits the parameters of the case."

"We're honored," LuAnn said, and Janice and Tess agreed. "So you said you felt like we needed to know this for our protection?"

"Not protection," he said. "More for your information. So you'll know how to respond if Marsha or Ellie returns."

"And what is it we should do?" Tess asked.

"Call me." Tom made circles in Agent Butler's lap and then plopped down. The agent began to rub the cat's head.

"That's it?" LuAnn asked.

"That's it." He shook his head. "As I said, I can't give you any details regarding why the witness went into our protection. I can, however, tell you she is testifying. The man she's testifying against is not likely a danger to you, only to her and to our marshal."

"I bet we've seen him," LuAnn said. "I bet it's that guy we saw her with the other day."

Agent Butler turned his attention to her, his expression unreadable. "When was this, and what did the man look like?"

LuAnn told him the same thing she'd told Officer Goggan. "That must be who it is, don't you think?"

The agent stared at her. Finally, he nodded. "I have no problem with you ladies considering that man as someone who does not need to be around here. I am neither confirming nor denying he has anything to do with this case, but I would like you to call me if you see him again."

"Do you want us to call the police as well?" Janice asked.

Agent Butler smiled in her direction as he continued to pet the cat. "I would prefer if you kept local law enforcement out of it. I assure you that my colleagues have a much faster reaction time."

"I see," Tess said. "What about those payments for the two suites where the women were staying? I've been getting a credit card payment daily from the same card, but I assume you knew that."

"Those payments will continue. Ellie and Marsha are aware that they have a place to stay until a certain date. That was the plan and will continue to be the plan."

"Until trial," LuAnn said. "Then she gets a permanent name change and a home and identity somewhere far away from wherever she has testified."

"Yes," he said. "It sounds like you've done your research, as I would expect."

"I have," she said softly. More than she would tell any of them, actually. From the time she first found out where her father had gone and why, LuAnn had not only researched the witness protection program and how it worked but had also tried her best to learn anything she could about her father, either before or after he went in. And though she had learned plenty about the program, she never found anything out about her father.

Until she received the letter.

The letter. LuAnn shook her head. "Agent Butler, I have a question. What will happen to the things that were taken from the inn and from Grant's studio? I have two very personal items missing, and I desperately want them back."

His expression softened. "I'm sorry, LuAnn," he said gently, "but anything we find cannot be returned. It will be logged in as evidence until the case is closed."

"But why?" Tess demanded.

"Goodness gracious goat. It's her father's letter and their last picture together," Janice said. "Is that too much to ask that those things be returned?"

"That's what you're so concerned that we return?" he asked LuAnn.

"The letter and picture that were hidden behind the framed photograph of a couple by the river." LuAnn shook her head. "They are my last link to my father, Agent Butler, and it hasn't been too long since it was sent to me. Both my mother and my father are gone now, and I can't imagine not ever having those two small links to my past again."

"I'm sorry," he said, and he did truly look as if he hated delivering that news. "I will do whatever I can to see that your items are returned once the case is closed, but I can't promise anything. If I could, I would."

Tess spoke up. "What if there was something *we* could do?"

He smiled. "Then I would hope that your methods were not illegal and that I would never find out about it."

"It's a deal," Tess said.

"Now, just one more thing," Agent Butler said. "We've been over everything that happened from the First Friday celebration through last night's astronomy gathering. However, looking back over all that time, does anything stand out as odd?"

"What do you mean?" Janice asked.

"I mean something that, when it happened, you wondered what was up. Like, was there an odd thing that a guest on Friday said or maybe was there someone in the astronomy group who looked a little strange?"

"Have you seen the astronomy group, Agent Butler?" Tess said dryly.

"Fair enough. But starting with Friday night, what comes to mind when I say the words 'that was odd'?"

"The food truck," LuAnn said suddenly.

Agent Butler shifted positions to look at her. "What about the food truck was odd?"

"First off, there was more than one. We had a truck catering for us at First Friday in the back by the loading dock, but there was another one parked out front. It was a seafood-themed truck as best I remember. Brad and I went over to investigate, but they took off."

"Brad?" he said. "Would that be Brad Grimes, the Realtor?"

"Yes," LuAnn said. "Then there was another truck on Monday that offered Mexi-ribbean grilled cheeses, whatever those are. I remember commenting that it sounded interesting, but it drove away before we could investigate."

"Is it unusual to have food trucks on your street?"

"This is the first I've seen them." LuAnn paused. "But I did ask Brad if he thought it was strange that we suddenly were so popular with the food trucks. He said he recalled there was something on the city council agenda about creating a park for food trucks nearby. He suggested they might be scoping out the area to see if they were interested in participating."

Agent Butler nodded but didn't offer comment. He did, however, make a note in his notebook.

"Oh!" Tess said. "Remember when another food truck was parked out front, and I went out to speak to them because I thought they were the caterers we hired for First Friday?"

Tom shifted positions on Agent Butler's lap and nudged his hand to remind him to continue petting him. "What happened when you went out to speak to them?"

"They took off before I could get close enough to say anything."

"Maybe they didn't see you," he said as he complied with Tom's demands.

"It's possible. I thought it was a little odd then, but now I think maybe it's very suspicious. What do you think?" Tess asked.

"I think if I was inundated with food trucks that didn't want to sell me any food, I would call that suspicious." He paused. "Anything else?"

LuAnn sat back and listened while the others talked about a few of the guests and how they did things that were strange or caused attention. When it was her turn, she shrugged. "Other than having to let the dog out of Janice's room one day, I can't think of anything."

Agent Butler asked her to recount that story, and she did. When she was done, he smiled. "Thank you. You've been very helpful. If you think of anything else, call me on my cell."

"Agent Butler," LuAnn said as he set Tom aside and stood. "Where is Marsha?"

He gave her a startled look. "Why do you ask?"

"Because I think Ellie is the culprit and Marsha was the one assigned to protect her."

"Yes," Janice said. "I think LuAnn is right. I mean, if I had to spend my days trying to keep that woman in line, I would be grumpy too."

Tess leaned forward. "You're not going to answer that, are you?"

"I cannot confirm or deny any of it," he said. "However, rest assured that the FBI takes care of its own and takes care of those who help us." He smiled. "Which is why I want you three to be reassured that we are also doing our best to take care of you."

Later, when they were alone and the agents had gone downstairs to continue their investigation by interviewing Robin and Winnie in the kitchen, Tess rose and began to pace.

LuAnn sighed. "I know it's late, and I'm tired, but that's a lot to take in. I'm grateful that they trust us enough to send WITSEC participants here when they can."

"Yes, Agent Butler is a good man doing a hard job," Tess said. "But I refuse to allow you to just sit back and agree to give up your prized possessions. He didn't tell us not to look for them, he just said to be legal and not to tell him." She stopped in front of Janice's chair. "So what do you say?"

"I say I agree," Janice confirmed.

They both turned to look at LuAnn. "Well?" Tess asked, one brow lifted. "How about a legal and not-meant-for-FBI-knowledge search for a couple of lost items?"

"Whatever you're planning," LuAnn said, "count me in."

"Okay," Tess said. "First we need to decide how we're going to handle the others. Robin, Winnie, and Brad and Grant obviously know the FBI has become involved in the search for Ellie and Marsha. What are we going to tell them?"

"We can tell them that we're helping them collect the list of names," Janice offered, "but what we won't mention is that we'll be checking out everyone on that list to see if they might have helped Ellie steal LuAnn's picture."

"How are we going to do that?" Tess asked.

"Old-fashioned police work." Janice shrugged. "They do it all the time on television. We follow the leads and do some legal snooping on the people on the list. What do you think?"

"I think it's both amazing and terrifying that a pastor's wife has become so good at covert operations planning," Tess said with a giggle. "And I love it."

"I love it too," LuAnn said.

"Okay so that's us," Janice said. "What will you be doing, LuAnn?"

"If I beg off helping with the list that Agent Butler wants because I'm busy planning Thorn and Beverly's wedding," LuAnn said, "I can use that as an excuse to escape the inn and do some investigative work of my own."

"That's good," Tess said. "You can do the legwork under the guise of wedding planning details. What do you think?"

"Yes, I think that's a good plan."

Janice looked at each of them. "Do you think that will be enough to fool the Grimes brothers should they ask what you're up to? Last I saw, they were hanging out down in the café. I doubt they've left unless the agents forced them to. You can bet that one of us will get a call asking for the details."

LuAnn shrugged. "Grant, probably. But Brad? Doubtful. However, if we tell Brad there are things we're not free to explain, it's likely he'll honor that."

"He's a smart man," Janice said. "He'll figure it out on his own without any of us saying a word."

"I agree," Tess said. "And to borrow Agent Butler's words, just don't confirm or deny anything, and you'll be fine."

LuAnn laughed. "I think I can do that." She sobered. "The question is whether I try to do this alone or involve Brad, without telling him anything I'm not supposed to tell him, of course."

"My vote is to involve Brad," Janice said.

"Right," Tess said. "You absolutely do not need to do anything like this alone."

"True. I don't want to deceive him," LuAnn said. "And I do think that if we find Ellie, we'll find my valuables."

May 6, 1860

With dawn newly broken, Prudence folded her hands, eyes closed in her favorite spot on the porch. The early morning quiet settled around her as she allowed the words of King David's psalm to take hold of her heart. Yesterday word had come to them from town that a man had arrived with a camera and was setting up shop to take photographs.

Prudence's first thought was that she and Jason and Moses ought to pose for him. She would love nothing better than to preserve an image of the three of them for the future, for she surely had the handsomest husband and the most beautiful child in all of Marietta.

Prudence frowned. Pride, all of it.

"'Let not the foot of pride come against me, and let not the hand of the wicked remove me,'" she whispered.

Today King David's warning from the thirty-sixth Psalm surely did pierce her. How often had pride gotten her into more trouble than any enemy could have managed? She opened her eyes and allowed her gaze to wander through the expanse of trees down the river that flowed lazily past. Then she took up her journal and began to write.

Just like that river, I've held many secrets for longer than I can recall. Smooth waters hide dangerous depths, and a quiet life hides many a dangerous undertaking. Though good reason and circumstance has caused me to hide who I am and what I do, my Father in heaven knows all and sees all. He is not surprised by the man with the camera. What will that reveal if it is turned on me? If it is turned on us? What if we are discovered?

She stopped to look down at what she had just written. "Where is thy faith, Prudence?" she whispered. "Why fear now?"

If a man making photographs could so easily upend years of good works done in the name of the Underground Railroad, then only the Lord could save them all from that. She tore the page from the diary and set it aside to burn.

Later Jason came to sit beside her. "Thee was up late with Moses, and yet thee still rises with the sun."

"It is habit," she said. "And he is fine. Just his teeth coming in."

Jason stretched and took a sip from his mug. "We'll be making a trip into Marietta this morning," he told her. "The professor has arranged a meeting with a friend."

"Then thee will not need Moses and me there," she said.

"But I will."

"And why?" she asked him with a sideways look, her thoughts on the fussy child whose emerging teeth were giving him trouble.

"It is a surprise," he told her. He stood and kissed the top of her head. "We'll take the wagon."

"The wagon?" She shook her head. "But we always walk to town. Are we making a purchase?"

"We are not," he called from inside the farmhouse.

Prudence followed him in. "Thy leg is plaguing thee worse, is it not?"

He glanced over his shoulder. "Whether it is or it isn't, we will still be taking the wagon."

She considered. Jason could be stubborn, this much was true, but he was her husband, and she would not change a thing about him, stubbornness or not.

A few hours later, the wagon halted in front of Marietta College. The college was an impressive pair of buildings facing the street with a chapel set between them. Rhett Ashworth came bounding out of the building on the left and hurried toward the wagon.

When he spied Prudence, he paused to tip his hat. "A good day to you, Mrs. Willard," he said.

"A good day to thee, Professor Ashworth," she replied as she watched him climb into the back of the wagon.

At the professor's instruction, Jason pulled the wagon around to the back and stopped there. He and the professor left the wagon in Prudence's care and hurried inside the building.

Prudence bounced Moses on her knee, one hand holding the reins. The door reopened, and Jason hurried out. The professor and another man, a tall fellow with a shock of dark hair and a suit that was too short in the sleeves, followed just behind him. The stranger carried a wooden box with a funnel attached on one end, while Professor Ashworth held a stick with three legs attached. They deposited the items in the back of the wagon, and then went back inside, returning with a trunk that, with difficulty, was placed beside the stick and box. They moved two more trunks the same way, slowly and with difficulty. Once more they went inside and returned with a trunk, this one smaller and apparently lighter.

Once all of the items were loaded in the back of the wagon, Jason came around to introduce Prudence. As Jason spoke, Prudence realized this was the man who took photographs. The very man who caused her to tackle the issue of pride this morning.

"Prudence?" Jason said. "Did thee hear me?"

She shook her head. "Oh, I'm terribly sorry."

"There is nothing to apologize for," the man said. "My name is Jefferson Inman. I have a son of my own who is just about your son's age. You've got a fine-looking boy, Mrs. Willard."

"Thank thee, Jefferson," she managed. "So thee is the man with the camera that everyone is talking about?"

"Guilty," he admitted. "I never expected to make a stop here in Marietta, but then I also never expected to stumble upon a meteorite the same day it fell. Did you see it?"

"We did," Prudence said.

"Fascinating to watch. I was aboard the steamer *Victory* when we all saw it. The captain headed to port immediately, and I have been landlocked ever since. Not that I am complaining. Matthew will be beside himself when he sees the photographs I have taken."

"Matthew Brady," Professor Ashworth supplied. "Have you heard of him?" When Jason indicated he had not, the professor continued. "He's a New York fellow. Sends men like my friend Jefferson here to take photographs all over the country."

"If we go to war," the photographer said, "we'll all be summoned back to take photographs of the soldiers. Until then, we're working out in the field. Which occasionally means I get to see old friends."

The professor grinned. "Shall we get on with it, then?"

The men climbed into the back of the wagon and held the box camera between them while Jason set the wagon in motion again. A few minutes later, they were headed northeast along an unfamiliar trail that seemed to follow the Muskingum River.

"Where are we going?" she asked Jason as the wagon rocked along.

"It will become apparent soon enough," he said softly. "Just know anything I have done or will do is for thy protection. And for the protection of our son."

CHAPTER NINETEEN

The women joined Brad and Grant in the kitchen for an early supper. After cleaning up, they got out of Winnie's hair and retired to the long harvest table in the café, coffee cups in hand.

"So," LuAnn said to the men, "I suppose you've been briefed on the excitement?"

"*Brief* would be the key word here," Grant said as he exchanged looks with Brad. "We have been told very little, but we have a few theories."

"We do," Brad said, "but I would like to hear anything you might be able to tell us."

LuAnn sighed. "I'm afraid there isn't a lot that I can tell. Ellie and Marsha are missing, and because of that, the FBI is now involved. I was told in no uncertain terms that they are looking for the people and not anything we might have lost."

"Man," Grant said, "that's a bummer about losing your camera."

"And your negatives," LuAnn added.

"That too," he said. "But to tell you the truth, I'm having such a good time with this tintype camera that I don't miss starting over. It would be nice to have those pictures back, but I can always create more."

LuAnn felt Brad's eyes on her and turned toward him. He continued to watch her intently.

"So," she finally said, "were you two interviewed by the agents, or have you been waiting for one of us?"

"Both," Brad said. "Apparently we were spotted down the street from Ellie's new place. Because we got there before the Feds, that raised a few questions. I explained that you and I had just left the police station after meeting with the sketch artist, and we figured we would go and see if Ellie had simply moved out of the inn and into the rental without remembering to check out."

"And?"

"And the agent listened and wrote it all down." He shrugged. "Beyond that I have no idea if my face is now on a do-not-trust list somewhere in Washington, DC or what."

"It's a nice face," Grant said with a grin, "even if it is kind of wrinkled around the eyes."

"So funny." Brad grinned at his brother, then turned his attention to LuAnn. "I'm curious why you ladies were up there with the FBI agent so long, but I doubt you can tell me."

LuAnn smiled. "I can tell you that part of the time was spent catching up on Agent Butler's twins and watching him pet the cat in his lap."

"Tom? I didn't think that cat liked any lap other than yours and the two other innkeepers'."

"I know," she said. "Apparently Tom likes him."

"So now that we've dispensed with that, what else can you tell me?"

She paused. "As I said, the basic issue with the FBI doing all of the legwork on this case is that they can only look for our missing guests. Finding our lost items is not exactly at the top of their to-do list. Agent Butler told us to stay out of their way if we wanted to keep looking for the things that were taken. We were warned that whatever we did, it had to be legal, and he'd better not find out."

"That covers a lot of territory," Brad said.

"It does." She wrapped her hands around her mug. "Imagine being told by the FBI that they don't want to find out what you're up to."

Brad nodded and rested his palms on the table. "That leaves us with a big question, then. What do we do to get your camera and Grant's negatives back?"

"And my photograph," LuAnn said. "Actually, that is the most important thing of all." She shook her head. "I'm sorry. Let me rephrase that. The negatives are very important even if Grant believes they are replaceable. The reason I want that photograph back is a sentimental one. As much as I loved it, it's what I had hidden behind it that is irreplaceable to me."

"What is that?" Brad asked.

How many times would she have to recount this loss out loud? She paused to collect herself. "Mementos from my late father," she decided to say, shortcutting the process of describing exactly what those mementos were.

"So you put things behind the picture in the frame?" Grant asked. "Why?"

"Don't be so nosy," Brad said, putting his hand on LuAnn's. "It's none of your business why."

"No, I don't mind answering him." She turned her attention to Grant, whose blue eyes and dimples made him unmistakable as a relative of Brad's. "I had a good conversation with someone with experience in grief counseling. She understood. It's important to me that you understand."

"Go on," Brad told her, his hand still atop hers.

"The things I hid behind the photograph were reminders of a man whose life I mostly missed due to his absence. I didn't know if he was alive or dead until not that long ago. What I placed behind the photo was my last connection to him. I wanted it nearby but not visible. To know it was there was a comfort, but to look at it was painful at times."

"Then we need to find this photograph and get these things back for her, Brad," Grant said.

"I agree." He rose. "First order of business is to go back out to Ellie's rental and see if maybe she's returned. If the Feds have gone, we can get out of the car and poke around a little. If not, we call it a night and figure out another plan tomorrow. What do you say?"

LuAnn gave him a look. "How did you know I was about to say that?"

He offered his hand to help her to her feet. "Great minds think alike. Besides, what better time to do a little investigating of our own than under cover of darkness? Now grab your purse and let's go."

A short while later, LuAnn suppressed a shiver as dark clouds rolled past the moon, deepening the darkness.

"Chilly?" he asked.

"A little," she said with a half-smile. "I was fine until I ran out of coffee."

He reached into the back seat and grabbed his leather jacket and handed it to her. LuAnn snuggled into the warmth, inhaling the masculine scent of soap and the aftershave she knew was his favorite. Had she not been on a stakeout, she could have happily curled up and taken a nap within the comforting folds.

Brad had checked his phone three times but said nothing. Finally he smiled when his phone dinged. "Okay," he said. "It looks like we might be able to get in. I texted the number that Ellie gave Grant, and she responded."

"She did?" LuAnn was wide awake now. "Are you serious? You just got a response from the woman that half of law enforcement in Ohio is looking for?"

Brad turned the phone toward her to show LuAnn the text. Indeed, there was a message from Ellie giving Brad permission to enter the garage to pick up the Grimes Realty rental sign. She also asked him to go into the house to check to be sure the punch list had been completed by the handyman.

"Wow," LuAnn said. "How easy was that?"

He grinned. "I know. It's almost too easy."

A red pickup truck roared past at high speed, cutting off any further conversation. The truck's brake lights went on, and he turned in to Ellie's driveway.

"Déjà vu all over again," LuAnn said.

"Only without Suburbans." Brad shook his head. "I think that truck belongs to Justin."

LeAnn leaned forward and squinted her eyes to get a better look at the driver. He seemed to be holding up his cell phone, though from this distance she couldn't be certain.

"I wonder why he's here," she said.

"Maybe the FBI paid him a visit," Brad suggested. "It would make sense that they would call on the owner of the last place Ellie was suspected to be."

"If indeed she ever actually moved in," LuAnn said. "I mean, just because she signed the lease, that doesn't mean she actually moved anything in. All she had as far as I know were suitcases, even though she mentioned that her wedding planning supplies were in transit from Savannah."

"Who knows?" Brad nodded toward the truck. "Look, Justin's getting out. Looks like he's heading toward the garage. Maybe the Feds asked him to come over here for some reason."

"I guess that makes sense," she said. "Should we go see what he's up to?"

"Sure." Brad opened his car door and started to get out.

LuAnn opened her door. "But after this, I want a big cup of hot chocolate."

A roar rolled past, shaking the car and causing the windows to shudder. A split second later, a plume of black smoke rose above the little house on Cherry Street.

Her eyes on the smoke and her heart racing, LuAnn paused. *Father, please wrap your arms around Justin and keep him safe.*

"Call 911," Brad shouted as he threw off his seat belt and bolted out of the car. "Tell them what just happened, and be sure they know there's the possibility of a fireman down. Justin O'Hara's guys are probably going to be the first responders on the scene. They need to be warned."

LuAnn managed to get her phone out of her purse as Brad raced down the street toward the burning house, but typing the three numbers with her shaking fingers was nearly impossible. She finally managed to succeed on the third try.

Though she felt like all she could do was babble answers, somehow the dispatcher understood. "You say you saw Justin O'Hara go in right before you saw the explosion?" he said. "Our Justin from the fire station near downtown?"

"Yes, that's the one," she told him. The smoke had thickened, and the plumes seemed to reach twice as far into the sky. Flames were now shooting out of the attic windows, and Brad had disappeared from sight.

"Hurry, please," she managed. "Brad Grimes has gone to see if he can help."

"Before or after the explosion?"

Another crash of sound and flames rattled the car. LuAnn fumbled with the seat belt with her free hand as she held tight to the phone.

"Both," she shouted. She climbed out of the car and ran.

"Ma'am," the dispatcher shouted into her ear. "Was that a second explosion?"

"Yes," she shouted over the sound of the roaring flames. "Justin went to the garage before the first one, and Brad went to check on him right before the second one. I'm trying to find them, but the smoke is too thick."

A screaming siren broke the silence. A second later the sound grew closer, and flashing red lights caught her attention.

The firefighters were coming. Or maybe it was police. Or the Feds. But none of that mattered. LuAnn kept running.

She found Brad on the sidewalk behind Justin's truck. His eyes were closed, and his face, hair, and clothing were covered with a dusting of black ash.

"Brad!" she shouted. "Brad, talk to me!"

No response.

Immediately LuAnn's first aid training kicked in. She tucked Brad's jacket around him and pressed her shaking fingers to his neck to check for a pulse. Before she could determine anything, someone pulled her away.

"No," she shouted only to realize a pair of EMTs had taken over and were working on him.

"Where's Justin?" one of the firemen called.

"We saw him get out of his truck and go toward the garage," she shouted over the sound of sirens and the roar of the fire. "I don't know if he got inside before the first explosion or not."

A third roar split the air, and then everything went dark.

CHAPTER TWENTY

All LuAnn could hear inside the darkness was a persistent ringing. Then she heard a voice calling her name, and opened her eyes to see Officer Goggan kneeling beside her.

"She's awake," he said to someone behind him, his voice barely registering over the sound in her ears.

LuAnn tried to sit up but found her arms would not cooperate. Officer Goggan put a hand on her shoulder.

"You're going to be fine," he said. "But don't try to sit up until a paramedic has checked you out."

She looked up at him. "What happened?"

Then it all came back. The red truck. Justin. The explosion. Brad.

"Where's Brad?" she said as she scrambled to her feet. "He was right there on the ground and..." She spied him sitting in the back of the ambulance and raced toward him, not caring that her legs were unstable and her ability to walk a straight line completely nonexistent.

"Hold on there." She heard Officer Goggan follow her. "You haven't been seen by the EMT yet."

LuAnn shrugged him off. "Except for the fact that I'm hearing more bells in my head than were present at Marla Still's wedding, I am fine."

She paused at the back of the ambulance and looked at Brad. He was sitting up on the gurney with a blanket and his jacket wrapped around his shoulders.

"Hey there," he said as he turned in her direction.

"Hey there," she echoed as cheerily as she could manage.

Brad nodded at the EMT and the string of IVs behind him. "If you're hungry, this guy is offering a smorgasbord of spiked appetizers, but no solid food."

The EMT shook his head. "Grimes, when you start telling bad jokes, that's when I kick you out of my ambulance."

Brad grinned and threw off the blanket, then rose to shake the EMT's hand. "Exactly the exit I was looking for. See you this weekend for the basketball game at the Y?"

"Humor me, and wait at least until next week. The Gray Geezers can lose just as well without you as they can with you."

"The Gray Geezers?" LuAnn lowered her eyebrows at him. "Really?"

"Really," he told her. "And before you tease me about the name, it isn't just my hair that got me onto the team."

"That's true," the EMT said. "We let him play with us because he paid for the uniforms."

"Technically, Grimes Realty did," he said with a chuckle. "It's a write-off."

"Next season I think maybe Grimes Realty needs to pay for free-throw lessons." He fended off Brad's response with a wave of his hands. "All joking aside, remember the head injury protocol I told you about, and do not show up at practice or a game for at least a week."

"Yeah, got it. Next weekend and head injury protocol. Check." He shook hands again with his friend, then strolled over to LuAnn. He draped his jacket back over her shoulders.

LuAnn searched his face. "When I saw you lying behind the truck I thought..." She couldn't say it.

"I think that fall backward from the explosion stunned me for a minute. I remember hearing you and wanting to open my eyes, but I couldn't. I seem to be fine now, except that I can barely hear over the ringing in my ears."

"Me too," LuAnn said. The scream of a departing ambulance split the night, and LuAnn pressed her palms to her ears. Then she remembered.

"Justin?"

"In the ambulance. I don't know the details, but the first explosion knocked him backward and threw a massive Grimes Realty sign on top of him. The sign we should have picked up two days ago might have saved his life."

"Might have?" LuAnn asked.

"EMTs say he's going to be fine because the sign covered him and protected him from the blow and the fire when the other two bombs went off."

LuAnn pulled her phone from her pocket. "I've got to call the girls and tell them to get to the hospital to see how Justin is. We can meet them there when we're done here."

A ruckus of lights and noise arose at the edge of the field of police cars. A television crew, complete with lights and cameras, pushed their way as near as they could to the scene.

LuAnn recognized the news anchor from the local station but had no intention of allowing him to catch her on camera. She moved to a spot behind the open door of the ambulance and tucked Brad's jacket up close against her face while she talked to Tess.

"Brad, thank goodness you're okay!"

LuAnn looked over to see Brad motioning for Marissa to move past the perimeter tape and come over to him. Notebook and press badge in hand, she jostled past the policeman to fall into Brad's arms. LuAnn wound up her call. "Tess, I'll see you at the hospital. I've got to go *now.*"

After a moment, Marissa held Brad at arm's length. "When I heard the chatter on the police radio, I couldn't believe it was you. I was terrified and I—"

"Marissa," he said evenly, "you remember LuAnn, don't you?"

She turned, seemingly surprised to see LuAnn there. "Yes, of course. How are you?"

"Glad to be alive, thank you," LuAnn said. "Brad, would you take me to the hospital, please? I want to check on Justin."

"Of course I will." Brad disengaged himself from Marissa's grasp.

"Not just yet."

They all turned to see Agent Butler walking toward them. "Whom do I have the honor of thanking for getting me all the way back here tonight?"

LuAnn raised her hand. "That would be me, I suppose."

Brad moved between her and the FBI agent, Marissa still trailing him. "I'm guilty as well."

"Miss Sherrill, Mr. Grimes, would you do me the courtesy of joining me over there in my mobile office?" He nodded to the Suburban parked just beyond the television lights.

Marissa followed several steps behind Brad until Agent Butler moved between them. "Excuse me, why are you following us?"

She looked to Brad to respond, and then shrugged. "I'm here to check on my friend."

"And get an insider statement you can run in tomorrow's paper." He shook his head and pointed to the yellow crime tape. "Neither is going to happen. Please see yourself out of my crime scene."

Marissa's mouth opened, but she seemed to be having trouble forming a response. Finally she nodded and trudged away.

"I'm sorry," he told Brad, "but your girlfriend needs to remain out there with the other civilians."

"She's not my girlfriend," he protested as he helped LuAnn into the Suburban.

"She wants to be," LuAnn said before she could stop herself. The comment was catty at best, and she couldn't believe she'd said it. "I'm sorry. That wasn't nice," she quickly amended before Brad closed the door. He then ran around the back to take the seat beside her.

Agent Butler climbed into the passenger side of the Suburban and turned around to face them. "Okay, LuAnn, my guess is you and your friend here both are having hearing problems. Bells ringing, perhaps?"

They nodded.

"That's what happens when you're near enough to the explosion to feel the percussion. It will knock you backward." He turned his attention to Brad. "As you discovered the hard way."

He fiddled with some knobs on the dash. "Full disclosure. I have a recording device set up in here. It saves me from taking notes, and I have the advantage of getting fresh statements. So, who wants to tell me what happened?"

LuAnn looked at Brad, and nodded. "I vote he does."

Brad let out a long breath. "All right, but let me preface this by saying that I will neither confirm nor deny that LuAnn and I were intending to stop by Ellie's new rental and pick up the sign that my brother put in the yard when he signed the listing agreement with Justin."

"Cute," Agent Butler said. "Go on."

"LuAnn and I were just getting ready to get out and decide what our next step would be when a red truck flew past at a high rate of speed."

As Brad continued to give his account, LuAnn sat back and listened. When he reached the part where the second explosion knocked him flat, she began to shake. By the time he finished his story, her teeth were chattering. She wrapped Brad's jacket around herself and tried not to attract any attention.

The attempt failed miserably.

"Has she been checked out?" Agent Butler asked Brad.

"You can talk to me," LuAnn said. "I'm right here."

"She has not," Brad told him. "At least not to my knowledge."

The agent pressed a button on his earpiece and said something quietly. A moment later, his associate was at the wheel and the Suburban was in motion.

"I'm fine," she protested.

And she continued that protest all the way to the emergency room, into the exam room, and afterward when the doctor prescribed bed rest and head injury protocol.

"Hey," Brad said with a beaming smile as they walked into the ER waiting room, "I got head injury protocol too. It's like we're twins."

"Borrowing a statement from your buddy the EMT, when you start telling bad jokes…"

He shrugged. "Okay. The party's over anyway. Looks like my ride is here."

Grant came over to them, his expression grave. "I risked speeding tickets to get to the hospital, and I find you hanging out with LuAnn and cracking jokes."

"Oh, he started that way back in the ambulance," LuAnn told him.

At Grant's confused expression, Brad shook his head. "Never mind. Let's go." He turned to LuAnn. "I still owe you that coffee."

Tess and Janice burst through the waiting room door, wild-eyed. They slowed when they saw LuAnn and Brad upright and whole. Janice was clutching LuAnn's purse. "Officer Goggan grabbed this from Brad's car before they towed it to the police yard to be checked over. He insisted it not be included in the roster of crime scene items."

"Thank you," LuAnn said as she held her purse to her chest. "I'm so grateful. You absolutely have no idea."

"Wow," Janice said. "I had no idea you were so attached to this purse."

"It isn't the purse I'm attached to," she said. "It's the notebook that's inside of it." She retrieved her precious notebook and smiled. "I cannot imagine trying to finish planning Thorn and Beverly's wedding without this."

"Oh no you don't," Tess said as she pulled out her car keys. "You will do nothing of the sort. Head injury protocol does not allow for wedding planning. We will simply call Tie the Knot and let them take over. They're wonderful people and will do a fabulous job. Now let's get out of here."

"No we won't, Tess," LuAnn said. "As much as I have loved every wedding they have done, this one is special. I don't think I ever told you guys, but Thorn actually came by and asked me for advice on what to wear on his date with Beverly the night he proposed."

LuAnn slid the notebook back into her bag and shook her head. "No more discussion about Ellie or weddings tonight, okay? I'm so thankful that Justin's injuries are minor and that Brad and I had barely a scratch. Let's just dwell on that tonight and think about the rest of it tomorrow."

"Good deal." Tess ran out to the car to pull under the overhang of the Emergency Room exit.

The ladies piled in and set off for the inn with Janice in the front seat and LuAnn in the back. After a few minutes, Janice turned to face her. "That was terrifying," she said.

Tess glanced at LuAnn in the rearview mirror. "It was," she said. "We heard the explosion, and it sounded so close. Then you called and said Justin and Brad were injured, and I couldn't get to my purse and keys fast enough."

"The Lord protected all of us tonight," LuAnn said. "I just don't have any idea what Justin was doing there. He seemed to be in a hurry when he passed us, so I doubt it was a casual social call." She paused. "Do you think for some reason Ellie might have lured him there?"

Tess drummed her fingers on the steering wheel. "You mean she planted some bombs and wanted him at her house when they blew?"

Janice shuddered. "Why would she want to hurt Justin?"

Tess and LuAnn shook their heads. LuAnn pondered the question all the way back to the inn and came up with nothing but a headache for her efforts. That night, with Huck tucked in at her feet and Tom purring beside him, she lay awake and gave thanks for the Lord's protection.

As the moonlight filtered through the curtains and danced across the bedcovers, she let her mind wander, as she often did during that time between consciousness and slumber. Only then did she realize that the truth she had been learning in the *Praise before Panic* Bible study had served her well today.

She really had managed to praise rather than panic. LuAnn nestled beneath her blankets with a smile. There was still so much she could worry about in their current situation. But tonight the Lord had kept all of them safe.

"Thank You, Father," she whispered before she gave in to a sweet, sound sleep.

Sunday passed quietly. Tess and Janice insisted she rest, and she did—except for an hour or two in the afternoon. She called Saffron and asked her to come over with Prudence's quilt. Saffron shared the story with Tess and Janice, and they had a wonderfully sweet time, with much laughter and a few tears. The cure worked, for she woke up Monday morning with much less ringing in her ears and determined to get on with her day.

She consulted her calendar, then hurried downstairs to help with the breakfast service. "Oh no you don't," Janice protested. "Not today."

"Come on in here after you eat," Winnie called from the kitchen door. "They won't put you to work, but I will. You're a better soup cook than I am anyway. But first you have your breakfast. I won't have a hungry cook in my kitchen."

"You heard her," Janice said. "Give me a minute, and I'll get some breakfast and coffee for you."

"Seriously, I couldn't let you wait on me."

"Better to wait on you than to visit you in the hospital," Janice said. "Or worse."

LuAnn nodded. "Thank you, then." She visited with a couple passing through Marietta on a photography tour and felt a twinge of sadness that she couldn't show them Grant's beautiful pictures. Tess motioned her over to let her know that Justin was on the phone for her.

"Justin," LuAnn said. "I'm so glad to hear from you. And so glad you're all right."

"Mostly," he said. "My ears are ringing like crazy. Are yours?"

"They were pretty bad last night, but they're better today," she said. "Brad told me you were saved by the real estate sign."

"That's the story," he told her. "I called because I'm wondering why I passed you guys when I was heading to the house. What were you doing on Cherry Street?"

"Brad and I were just waiting for a bit to see if Ellie would show up. She hasn't checked out of the inn, but we haven't seen her since Wednesday night. The next thing we knew, you were flying past and then we saw smoke."

"I was flying past because Ellie called to tell me some kids had thrown rocks through my garage windows. The last thing I remember is getting out of my truck to go see the damage."

LuAnn frowned. "So Ellie wanted to harm you?"

"I guess so, only I didn't go in the house. When I walked up to the garage, it blew." He paused. "Arson squad thinks Brad and I triggered trip wires, but the thing that confuses me is how someone could get that place wired up so quick after the Feds were all over it."

"So you heard about that," she said.

"Everyone in town heard about that," he said. "My buddies in law enforcement were not happy when that dude from the FBI came in and took over. Apparently there's a US Marshal missing. I guess that's when the Feds get serious."

"Apparently so," she said. "So are you still at the hospital? If so, what can we bring you?"

"No, I'm home. The guys at the station are taking pretty good care of me." He paused. "But if you wanted to let it slip to Saffron that I'm lonely over here recuperating and could use someone to watch movies with and maybe order a pizza, that would be great."

LuAnn smiled. "I'll see what I can do."

"You're the best." He paused. "And hey, I'm glad you and Brad weren't hurt."

"So am I, but I'm very sorry that your house was destroyed. You worked hard on it."

"I did," he said. "I'm sure the arson guys will be making sure that what happened wasn't due to my workmanship. I hope that's not what it was."

"Justin, I doubt that very seriously, especially given the timing and how it all happened."

"Yeah," he said. "I guess we'll see. Now, about the pizza and movies?"

"And Saffron," she added as Grant walked in the door. "Right. I see her dad walking in right now. I'll be sure and mention it to him."

"Hey now, don't tease me," Justin said. "That dude doesn't want me dating his daughter."

"You're probably right," she said. "So maybe you ought to have pizza and movies with your buddies instead."

"You're no fun," he said with a laugh. "But, seriously. I'm glad you weren't harmed."

"Thank you," she said, then hung up to greet Grant. "I was just talking to Justin O'Hara. He's going to be fine."

"He's the one who's got a thing for Saffron, isn't he?"

She nodded.

"I'm glad he wasn't seriously hurt, but he's not going out with her as long as I have any say in the matter."

LuAnn shook her head. "Which you don't," she told him. "She's not a little girl anymore."

"Agreed, but that's not why I came in here. I was driving by, and there's three big black SUVs parked in front of your inn."

"What?" LuAnn pressed past him to see the intimidating vehicles parked across the street. "Tess! Janice!"

Her friends scrambled out of the kitchen and fell in behind her once she pointed out her destination. Armed with just enough irritation to push her forward, she crossed the street and banged on the closed door of the first vehicle.

The door opened immediately.

"Agent Butler," she said. "Have you found something? Why are you here?"

"Come in, ladies." He looked past her to Grant. "You stay right where you are."

"No," LuAnn said to Grant. "You go bring Justin O'Hara a pizza and settle your differences. It's the least you can do for an injured firefighter." She paused. "Besides, if he becomes your friend, what are the odds Saffron will be interested in him?"

"Brad is right," he said. "You're brilliant, LuAnn. Thank you. Catch you later."

CHAPTER TWENTY-ONE

May 6, 1860

After the better part of an hour, with Moses wailing from the bouncing and jolting, Jason stopped the wagon next to an empty steamboat dock. Nearby was a large barn that appeared to be in use as a gathering point for items grown on nearby farms to be shipped up or down the river.

With Moses now practically inconsolable, Prudence excused herself from the men to take a walk and calm him. By the time she returned with Moses asleep on her shoulder, the men were having an animated conversation at the back of the wagon.

When Jason noticed her and said something, the men all turned her direction. By the time she reached them, the photographer and the professor had assembled the camera and were aiming it toward the wagon.

"Come over here," Jason called to her.

She did as he asked and then realized the reason. Her heart sank. "Thee wants him to photograph us?"

Jason nodded. "He has offered. It would be rude to decline."

"I don't know," she said slowly. "Perhaps he could just photograph the wagon, or the river, or…" She knew Jason would not be moved, but she gave one more attempt. "Jason," she said softly, "do you think it is safe considering our other activities?"

"We are among friends." He nodded toward the dock. "A steamboat is expected any time, and Jefferson will be on it when it leaves. We are merely passing the time until then."

She looked closely at her husband. Something was wrong. "We are?" she asked.

"We are," he answered firmly.

Prudence put on a smile. "All right." She turned to the photographer. "Jefferson, perhaps you could photograph Moses by himself?"

"Of course," he said, "but he will need to be very still. Can he do that?"

Jason glanced at her. "He cannot unless he is sleeping as he is now."

"Then I suppose we will have to photograph all of you," he said. "Or just Mrs. Willard and the child."

"No," Jason said. "All of us, please."

Jefferson spent what felt like an inordinate amount of time preparing his camera for the photograph. First he put together the sticks to form a tripod and then settled the box camera atop it. After some work, with assistance from the professor and Jason, the camera was ready.

Jason stood beside the wagon with the sun shining into his face. Prudence situated herself beside him and then turned a still-sleeping Moses toward the camera. Following instructions not to move or even blink, she stared into the light until she thought she might never see clearly again.

"Thank you," Jefferson called. "I always take more than one, so please don't go far."

A rumbling noise sounded upriver, and the professor went to the dock to investigate. "Steamboat," he called.

"Thank Thee, Lord," Jason whispered.

"Jason," she said slowly, "something is wrong, is it not?"

"Not now," he said. "Later."

"All right," the photographer called. "Once more for the camera."

From behind him the sound of horses' hooves rang out. Professor Ashworth reached down to press his palm over the revolver strapped to his belt while Jason went to the front of the wagon.

"Jason?" she asked softly. "What is happening?"

"Go to the front of the wagon," he said. "No matter what, run toward the river and swim toward the steamboat if there is trouble."

She did as he asked as two men approached on horseback. Both men were of middle age and wore the attire of businessmen. Their horses were of fine quality, as were their saddles.

The professor walked toward the men and then stopped as if waiting for them to arrive. When the three met in the middle of the path, their voices rose in what she quickly ascertained was not a friendly discussion. Meanwhile, the photographer and Jason turned the camera around to face the three men.

"Come and speak to them, then," the professor said loudly as he swiveled to walk back toward the wagon.

The pair on horseback remained in place. It appeared they were arguing.

Finally the professor interrupted them. "Men," he called to Jason and Jefferson. "Would you explain to these fellows from Virginia that we are here to escort the photographer back to his boat after working with the college on document-ing the New Concord meteorite?"

"He's telling the truth," Jason called. "I have the proof here."

"I am willing to look at proof," one of the men said while the other fell silent.

"Then come and see it." Jason reached into his pocket and pulled out the rock he had given to Moses. "This is but one sample. The trunks are filled with the rest, but unfortunately they are locked."

The stranger climbed down from his horse and stepped forward to examine the rock before returning it to Jason. "How do I know you're telling the truth about those trunks? I see three big ones, and it just so happens we have lost three good slaves."

"Go ahead and try moving one," Jason said. "The rocks are heavy, though, so be careful."

The man gave Jason a look and moved around to the side of the wagon where he gave one of the trunks a shove. It didn't budge. He tried again with the same result. Then he met Prudence's gaze.

"Well, hello there, lovely lady," he said to her. "Are you with these men?"

Jason grasped the man's arm and whirled him around. "She is my wife. Do not presume to speak to her."

Prudence bit her lip to keep from crying out. Though Jason was a man without full use of his injured leg, he sometimes forgot this detail. Now, apparently, was one of those times.

The man's eyes narrowed, then slowly he took one step back and then another. "I mean no harm," he said. "I merely wish to regain my property."

"We have nothing that belongs to you," the professor said. "So go back to Virginia where the law does apply to you, for it does not here."

"It applies where I wish it to apply," the man said.

"Perhaps thee would like to explain that to the judge," Jason said. "We are meeting him here so he can personally view the rocks we've found. If thee feels thee has a claim against us, then please stay."

The stranger shook his head. "There is no need to speak to a judge. It isn't the rocks I want."

"Then there is a need for you and your friend to leave," Professor Ashworth said. "Do not think to return else I will be forced to tell the judge that you two were attempting to take my camera."

"As I said," the other man repeated, eyes wide, "there is no need. It isn't the camera we're after."

"Then go before the vessel docks." Jason nodded toward the photographer. "And to be sure thee does not return, our friend has made a photograph of thee and thy friend, which he will keep safe with him." He paused. "Does thee fancy thy face in a newspaper concerning such an act?"

"He's bluffing," the other man called from upon horseback.

"There is no bluff in that man's words. I work for Matthew Brady," Jefferson told them. "Have you heard of him? He resides in New York and is a friend of many high-placed men at the *New York Times* and other important newspapers. He will certainly be impressed that I was able to capture a photograph of vigilantes. You men may find yourselves circulating on the front pages of papers all over the country."

"There are no vigilantes here," the Virginian protested, though he made haste to climb back on his horse and leave along with his companion.

"Did thee manage a photograph?" Jason asked Jefferson quietly.

Jefferson grinned. "I did not. The light was wrong, and my camera refused to adjust to make a clear image. However, that man doesn't know that, does he?"

Jason and the professor joined the photographer in laughter. Prudence, however, was still too shaken to celebrate. She rested her head against her son and gave thanks to the Lord that the backs of the horses were quickly fading into the distance.

Once the men were gone, Jefferson packed up his camera and stowed it in the small trunk. Then, one by one, they unloaded the larger trunks and moved them to the docks where the steamboat crew loaded them. Then it came time to say goodbye.

"I will see that the photograph of your family is delivered back to Marietta when I can manage it," Jefferson said to Jason. "These things cannot be rushed, so expect that it may take some time." He paused. "You're a good man, Jason Willard. May the Lord continue to bless you."

"And thee," Jason replied. "Safe travels to thee."

Jefferson looked at Prudence. "Thank you for your patience with us today. I am looking forward to returning to Marietta someday, and my colleague Rhett has told me the most extraordinary thing. Is it true you have a trained goose? For if it is, I would very much like to photograph it."

Prudence grinned. "It is true," she said. "I would be happy to allow such a photograph, but I fear Patience has a mind of her own and may have an opinion about it."

"That I am willing to risk," he said with a chuckle.

While Jason helped Prudence and Moses into the wagon, Professor Ashworth walked with the photographer all the way to the end of the dock. They clasped hands once more before they said their goodbyes. Then the professor walked back toward them with a broad smile.

"Does she know?" he asked Jason, who shook his head. "Then perhaps you ought to be the one to break the news."

"What news?" Prudence said.

Jason sighed. "Those trunks filled with meteorites?"

"Yes," she said slowly.

"There were no rocks in them." He looked over at the steamboat as it signaled its departure. "And it was no coincidence that there were three of them."

"Amos, Thomas, and Mary?"

"Yes," Jason said with a nod. "We slid Mary's in the middle in case of a situation just like the one that occurred. Her trunk would have been light compared to the trunks containing the much heavier men."

"Oh," she said softly, her feelings in a tangle.

Jason gave her a penitent look. "I am sorry we could not tell thee. The professor felt it important that if we were caught, thee could truthfully proclaim ignorance as to the contents and avoid prosecution."

"But I would not wish that thee alone took the blame, Husband," she managed.

"And I would not wish our son to lose both a mother and a father to prison or worse. Would thee?"

"No," she managed. "And yet…"

Professor Ashworth nodded. "It was Jason's idea to use the steamboat as their means of escape. We've known the owner was close behind them. That is why I was in that boat with you on the night of the rescue, although until I saw you there I had no idea the second person on the mission that night would be my friend's wife."

"And that is also why we had to have a plan that was out of the ordinary means we use for escape," Jason added. "We do not generally use steamboats, but this one is owned by a captain who is friendly to our cause."

The professor looked past them toward the river. "Like as not, Amos and his grandchildren are already making themselves comfortable and will soon be dining well and enjoying a protection we could not offer them here."

Jason and the professor fell into conversation as they turned the wagon back toward Marietta. While the men spoke of rocks and weather, of politics and horses, Prudence watched the road ahead and thought of Amos. Of Thomas and Mary and the lives they would lead when they reached their new homes. Of the families they would have and the past that would someday be so far behind them that it would no longer chase them.

And she held Moses just a little tighter.

CHAPTER TWENTY-TWO

"Y̲ou seem to be everywhere lately," LuAnn told Agent Butler as they sat together in the SUV. "Maybe you can tell us where Ellie is and why she wanted to kill her landlord."

"You'll have to excuse her, Agent," Tess said. "LuAnn always gets testy when she almost gets blown up."

He grimaced. "About that. We were so close." He shrugged. "We thought we had her, and then she slipped away. That's why we allowed all of you to get so close."

"I'm not happy about that," LuAnn said, her eyes narrowed.

"I was trying to flush her out by staging that raid on the house. It was all arranged to get her to come to the scene. We had people watching, but we never saw her. Apparently she was there, and we missed her."

"Apparently." LuAnn took a deep breath and let it out slowly. "Why was she trying to kill Justin?"

"I don't know yet," he said.

She straightened her spine and looked past Agent Butler to her friends. "Then we will just have to figure that out. Come on, Inn Crowd. We have a job to do."

"Ladies, I'm sure I don't have to warn you about interfering in a federal investigation," he called as they followed LuAnn out of the vehicle. "Let us do our job. We have access to GPS, facial recognition software, and all the latest technology. We'll find them, don't worry."

"Or we'll find them first," LuAnn muttered under her breath.

Later that afternoon, when the lunch shift was over and the kitchen put back to ready mode, the trio brushed past Taylor in the café to climb the stairs. On the second floor, they ignored Robin's curious stare and continued upward until they reached their apartment.

LuAnn went to the teapot but changed her mind and retrieved her notebook before taking a seat on the settee beside Janice. Huck and Tom vied for a spot on her lap until Tom won. Huck went off to sulk and ended up in Tess's chair with her.

"All right," LuAnn said. "We have a missing US marshal and a mystery man who are connected to the missing woman who is supposed to testify. My guess is this guy is someone she is going to testify against. Either that or he's a boyfriend she cannot give up."

"What if he's both?" Janice said. "What if she thought she could testify against him and disappear, but she's changed her mind?"

"Or he won't let her," Tess offered.

"Those are questions we can't answer right now," LuAnn said. "But we do know one thing for sure. Ellie was determined that no one was going to see that picture that Grant took. The answer lies somewhere in that picture."

Tess groaned. "But what good does that do us? We don't have a print of it. Yours is gone, and so are Brad's negatives."

"Yes, but I know something that Ellie has no way of knowing." LuAnn held up her finger.

"What?" Janice leaned forward eagerly.

"The first time I saw that picture, last year, I knew I wanted a print of it. But I didn't see it in Grant's studio or in his real estate office."

"You didn't? Where was it?" Tess was bouncing in her seat.

"Someplace I'm sure Ellie never went." She grinned. "Let's give our friend Harry a call."

Tess stopped bouncing. "Harry? Harry Olson? You mean that picture is at the antique mall?"

"That's exactly what I mean. Give me five minutes, and I'll have a picture of that picture on my computer."

True to her word, LuAnn made the call, and a few minutes later checked her email. "It's here."

Tess and Janice joined her at the desk and watched as she downloaded the image and enlarged it. It was fuzzy, yes, but they were all convinced: the subjects in the picture were Ellie Miller and the man she called her brother.

"Okay, so now we know why Ellie stole the pictures and the negatives. But we still don't know who these people are or why they wanted to kill Justin." Janice sank into an armchair. "So where do we go from here? How do we find out who they really are?"

"Clearer photographs would be handy," Janice said. "Then we could use that facial recognition software Agent Butler was talking about. I've heard Stuart talk about using it in his ME work. Of course, he uses it on dead people, but still, the idea must be the same."

"Ellie was thorough," LuAnn said. "She managed to take away every photograph of—" She snapped her fingers. "Wait a minute. Maybe she didn't."

She turned back to her computer and brought up the file of the First Friday pictures. "Brad is just sure this Gino guy was here the night of the party. If he was, I'll find him."

She clicked through thirty or forty pictures and then... there. A perfect close-up.

"Got it," she said. "I think that will do very nicely." She faced Tess and Janice with a triumphant smile. "Ladies, all we need to do now is figure out which facial recognition software will work for us, and I think we just might be able to solve the puzzle."

Tess set Huck on the ground and went into her sitting room to retrieve her laptop. "I'll see what I can find out about facial recognition. I know there are a lot of hotels that use the software to screen out potential problem guests. I shouldn't have too much trouble finding one that would be applicable for our use."

"If that doesn't work, I can always call Stu," Janice said.

LuAnn went in search of a picture of Ellie. She was much easier to spot—the woman was everywhere. She copied and pasted the two pictures into one document.

"Bingo," Tess called. "I gave up and sent a message to a friend of mine who works at a hotel in Las Vegas. He just sent a link to something he thinks will work for our needs. I'm downloading it now."

LuAnn forwarded the pictures to Tess, and then walked over to stand by her laptop while she uploaded them. "Now if we just plug the photo in..."

After a few clicks, the software went to work. Tess looked up, beaming. "Isn't it amazing how a little ingenuity and some software can possibly solve a case?"

"It is," Janice said. "Can you imagine even a generation ago trying to explain to our parents that we can put a picture into a machine and get a—"

"Oh no." Tess shook her head. "It came back with an error message. I'll call my friend in Las Vegas and see if he can talk me through troubleshooting this."

"Good idea." LuAnn glanced at her watch and frowned. "Oh, my. I lost track of the time. I've got a meeting with Laura and Beverly over at the church in less than half an hour."

"You go to your meeting," Janice said. "Tess and I will keep working on this here. We'll let you know the minute we find out anything."

LuAnn gave them a reluctant nod. She snatched up her purse and notebook, then headed over to Christ Fellowship Church, where she barely arrived before the bride and her daughter.

Paige walked briskly past as LuAnn stepped inside. "Be right with you," she said. "I knew you were coming this morning, so I decided to do my walking inside. Just one more lap, and I'll make my quota for now."

"All right," LuAnn called. She stepped into the sanctuary and allowed the feeling of deep peace to settle in her bones. The beauty of this simple but elegant church was only part of what made this place so sacred for her. A moment later, Beverly stepped inside and paused. She must have felt the same way.

"I'm so happy we're having our wedding here," she told LuAnn. "I can't imagine a better place to begin our second chance at a new life than here."

"Neither can I," Laura said. "It's absolutely beautiful just as it is, Mom. I wasn't sure I agreed with you not adding any flowers or bows here, but I think it's the right choice."

"As do I," LuAnn said. "Tell me what other decisions you two have made, so we can all be on the same page."

As the women discussed their plans, LuAnn made notes. Several times she stopped them to ask questions, but mostly she just let them talk.

Beverly smiled and rose as she focused on something at the back of the church. LuAnn followed her gaze and spied the reason for her smile.

Thorn had stepped inside, hat in hand. Any resemblance to the man who had lived hand-to-mouth in the upper rooms of the unrestored inn was gone. In his place was a handsome man who looked happier than LuAnn had ever seen him.

"I could marry you right here and right now," he said when Beverly closed the distance between them. "Honey, let's save LuAnn a whole boatload of trouble and just run off to the justice of the peace. It won't take ten minutes to get it all signed, sealed, and delivered, and then we can be off on our honeymoon."

"Oh no you don't," Laura said as she playfully scolded the couple. "Five more days, and your bride will walk down that aisle. You can wait." She shook her head. "Let me rephrase that. You *will* wait."

Thorn grinned. "Was she always this bossy, Bev?"

"Always," she said. "She reminds me a lot of you."

Suddenly feeling out of place in what was a beautiful family moment, LuAnn closed her notebook and reached for her purse. "I'm going to go ahead and leave you three to sort out your differences," she said with a grin. "But I'm with Laura. Give me five more days, and I promise I'll have a wedding for you that is worth the wait."

Thorn beamed as he held his beautiful red-haired bride-to-be in his arms. "Only thing worth the wait around here is this woman and our daughter. I waited a long time to be her husband again. Didn't think the Lord would ever allow it, but here He has, and He's given my little girl back to me too." He shook his head. "Seems like I've been waiting a lifetime. What's five more days?"

"I'm glad you feel that way, Dad," Laura said as LuAnn pressed past them to reach the door. "Because Mom and I want to talk to you about your tuxedo."

"Tuxedo?" Thorn frowned. "I never agreed to that. LuAnn, come back here and save me."

"No way," she said. "But if you're lucky, Paige will slow down enough on her next lap around the church building to come to your aid. Just be warned, we ladies are all probably going to agree with Laura and Beverly."

LuAnn stepped out into the midday sunshine and gathered her sweater close. The weather had gotten colder since she went inside, and the gray skies portended rain. Her phone rang, and she reached to answer it.

"We got it," Janice and Tess said.

"Why are you on speaker?" she asked. She held the rail with one hand and the phone with the other, then began to make her way down the stairs to the street.

"Because we got the software to work," Tess said. "Not only on the computer, but we also put it on our phones. And we're pretty happy about that." Huck barked in the background, and she laughed. "Huck's happy too, but I don't think Tom cares."

"Typical," LuAnn said. "So what did you find out?"

"Are you kidding?" Tess said. "We wouldn't think of doing this without you here. Hurry home."

LuAnn reached her car in record speed and drove back to the inn. When she got to the apartment, she found her friends sitting at the computer waiting impatiently.

"Okay, she's here," Janice said. "Press Send, and let's see what we find out."

"Come over here and bring your chair," Tess said. When LuAnn had complied, Tess clicked the Send button.

All three sat back to watch as the program's graphics kicked into gear. Triangles and circles and all sorts of other shapes danced across the screen as the photograph of Ellie and Gino remained in the center of the screen.

Then the dancing shapes stilled. One by one they marched off the screen leaving only the photograph.

"What's happening?" Janice said. "Isn't it working?"

"It is," Tess answered. "Remember what Bob told us? The shapes mean the program is searching. When the search stops, the program compiles the data and then spits out a report. We should be getting one about...now."

An icon popped up beneath each face on the screen with a clickable link that appeared to lead elsewhere.

"Okay," Tess said. "Moment of truth. Which one do we want to do first, Ellie or Gino?"

"Gino," Janice and LuAnn said in unison.

Tess clicked on his icon, and a name appeared: Eugene Winston. Only one additional listing came up. "Oregon Department of Corrections?"

"Click on it," LuAnn said. Instead of a list of identification documents, a number appeared.

"What is that?" Janice asked.

"I'm about to find out," Tess said. "We'll do this old school." She did a Google search for "Eugene Winston Oregon convictions" and came up with multiple pages. She clicked on the first one, a story with a headline that stunned LuAnn.

"He blew up a bridge," she said.

"With cars and people on it," Janice added.

"And his girlfriend, Amelia Sherwood, helped him." Tess shook her head. "Who is Amelia Sherwood?"

"Go back to the software and click on Ellie's link," LuAnn said. "I guarantee that's our Amelia Sherwood."

But it wasn't.

"I don't understand," LuAnn said. "Eugene is Gino. He was with Ellie. Brad and I saw him. How is it that she's not his accomplice? What are we missing?"

"Not what," Tess said. "Who?"

"I don't follow," LuAnn said.

"We're missing two people. Ellie and Marsha. Neither of them are Amelia Sherwood, but they're still missing. Ellie is connected to Gino. Gino blows up bridges, allegedly, and we believe Ellie was going to testify but is now on the run with him. And that's what we have so far."

Huck chose that moment to jump onto the settee, upsetting the notebook and sending it tumbling to the floor. The resounding thud frightened the little pup and caused him to skitter toward the ladies at high speed.

LuAnn caught him up in her arms and spoke softly to soothe him as she walked over to the settee. "Silly dog," she told him. "It's just my notebook."

Placing the pup on the cushion beside her, LuAnn reached down to retrieve her notebook. A couple of papers tumbled out of it and slid facedown across the smooth floor. Tess reached over to pick them up.

"Lu," she managed. "You need to see this." She handed the papers to LuAnn.

LuAnn turned the pages over, and there was the picture of her with her father, and her letter. "How did they get there?" she asked. "I never thought…"

Tears shimmered in her eyes, and LuAnn wiped them with the back of her sleeve. "Thank You, Lord. However You managed to do this, I am so much more than grateful."

CHAPTER TWENTY-THREE

The remainder of the week flew by as LuAnn busied herself with last-minute preparations for Thorn and Beverly's wedding. Now that the event was drawing near, Paige had ceased all efforts to have the baby early and was now doing just the opposite.

"I know I'll make it until after the wedding tonight," she said glumly as she adjusted the floral arrangement on the guest book table. "I was so sure the little one would be here a week ago. Two weeks ago, actually. My doctor said these things happen when they're going to happen, but, gracious! I thought it would have already happened. I mean, I have things to do, you know?"

LuAnn stifled a grin. "Now you're sounding like a pastor's wife."

She left Paige working on the decorations in the lobby and stepped into the church. There she found Thorn kneeling at the altar, his head bowed. Unwilling to interrupt him, she stepped back out and found her way to her car.

Back at the inn, she manned the phone as one by one the vendors checked in. With the reception being held in the café, the lunch service was shortened today. Winnie buzzed in and

234

out of the kitchen as she worked on the things she would be contributing to the event.

"And no food truck this time," she declared. "No more of that nonsense."

"It's not nonsense if it's all we have," Janice told her. "There was no way we would have interrupted your time away from the inn. You've been a rock, my friend. You deserved a vacation."

Janice's praise soothed the ruffled cook and got her back on track to finish the night's savory and sweet treats. She mustered Taylor and Robin and instructed them to do whatever Winnie commanded. With the kitchen now under control, the three friends turned to the café, where the tables would be decorated with tulle and ribbons, each with a centerpiece of flowers and candles.

"I never thought of myself as a crafty person," Tess said, "but this is kind of fun."

"*Kind* of fun?" Janice asked.

"Well, okay," she said. "I'm enjoying it. Now, if we had more tables than this or if I had to do this more than once in a blue moon...?" She shook her head. "Then it would not be fun."

"Ladies, this is perfect," LuAnn said when the last bow was tied and the last candle set in place, ready to light once the reception began.

With just enough time to bathe and dress for the ceremony, the ladies went upstairs. When LuAnn reached her sitting area, her cell phone dinged with a text from an unknown number: *Did you find them?*

Who is this? she typed back.

You did find them.

Again she asked who it was. This time the response was, *Ellie.*

"Tess, Janice," LuAnn called. "Come see this."

Where are you? LuAnn tapped in.

Safe.

LuAnn held out her phone so her friends could read the conversation. Then she typed, *I want to meet with you.*

Soon.

When?

No response. LuAnn typed the question again, and again there was no answer. She set her phone on her desk and shrugged. "I guess there's nothing else we can do right now."

"That's true," Tess said. "And we've got a wedding to attend."

"Yes, we do," Janice said. "I can't wait. I love weddings. Wasn't Marla's beautiful?"

"It was," LuAnn agreed. "But I think this one is going to be even better."

LuAnn hurried to dress and head for the church while the other two remained behind until just before the ceremony was to begin. When LuAnn spied them coming in, she ushered her friends to the back of the church and settled them into places where they could see everything. Just for a bit, she allowed herself a break to sit beside them.

A few minutes later, the pianist came in and began to play softly. As the music rose, Thorn and his groomsman—Grant— stepped into the church.

"I didn't know Grant was his groomsman," Tess said to LuAnn.

"I didn't either until the last minute," she said. "Thorn was being sort of secretive about it."

"That sounds like him," Janice said.

"Okay, well, I'm going back to see to Beverly. I'll join you after the bride comes in."

Just as Paige stepped up to the microphone and began to sing, LuAnn slipped out and headed down the hall to the bride's dressing room. There she found mother and daughter in an embrace. As she attempted to back out without interrupting the tender moment, Beverly looked up.

"Come in and join us," Beverly told her. "Laura was just praying."

"Please do," Laura said. "Mom asked me to pray for this second chance the Lord has given her. It's my honor to do so, but I sure would welcome some help."

"Yes," LuAnn said. "I would like that."

The three joined hands in a circle and were still in prayer when someone knocked on the door and called, "It's time."

They parted, and LuAnn offered Laura a tissue. Seeing Beverly needed one as well, she went for the box but found it empty. "I'll just go get another box from the ladies' room."

"It's fine," Beverly said as she reached behind her bouquet of white roses and retrieved a handkerchief. "Something borrowed," she said as she dabbed at her face. "And useful too."

Another knock, and this time Laura answered the door. "Tell them to start the music. Mama and I will be there."

LuAnn grinned. "All right. Showtime. I'm just going to scoot out of here. Laura, remember not to walk too fast. Beverly, take your time. Let everyone see that beautiful dress of yours."

She stepped out into the foyer and found Brad waiting for her. "What are you doing here?"

"Walking the bride down the aisle," he told her.

"Does she know?"

"I assume Thorn told her. If not, she's about to find out."

Just then Laura and Bev emerged from the dressing room. "What's this?" she asked Brad.

Brad shrugged. "Thorn thought you might want someone to walk you down the aisle. If you don't, I'll understand. If you do, then we probably ought to get going. The crowd is getting restless, and Paige hit a few high notes during her solo that made me wonder if she was having contractions."

"Oh no," Laura said. "Then let's go."

The music swelled, and Laura stepped out to walk down the aisle. They had chosen dresses in a lovely rust color that complemented Laura's subdued version of her mother's hair. Wearing pearls and carrying a bouquet of lilies, she looked every bit like the daughter of the bride and groom.

Then came Beverly, a vision in white, with a tulle headpiece and pearls that matched her daughter's. Brad walked slowly as he led her down the aisle to give her over to be remarried to Thorn.

LuAnn leaned against the doorframe, her heart soaring as the couple joined hands. The wedding was going absolutely perfect in every way. Pastor Ben opened his Bible and began to read. Beverly glanced at Thorn, and Laura beamed.

"LuAnn."

She turned around to see Paige standing behind her. "I know the timing is terrible, but would you possibly be able to give me a ride to the hospital?" she said quietly.

"Hospital?" LuAnn glanced into the church and then back at Paige. "Now?"

"Now."

Later LuAnn would wonder how she ended up standing in a delivery room rather than a reception room, but for now all she could do was help her friend as best she could until the actual birth coach could arrive. By the time the pastor stepped into the birthing room, his good suit now covered in a hospital gown, the wedding was over and the reception was in full swing.

She tossed her hospital gown in the hamper outside the birthing room and picked up her phone to call the inn.

Tess answered on the second ring. "Boy or girl?" she shouted as the sound of laughter and music flowed behind her.

"Neither yet," LuAnn said. "But it should be soon. I just wanted to let you know I'm on my way. How is it going so far?"

"Great," Tess said. "Everyone is having a great time, but Winnie isn't happy that you supplemented her cooking with that food truck. I thought we agreed no food trucks."

"Tess," she said slowly. "What food truck?"

"The one with the desserts. I think it's called Sweet Sue's Stuff and Things. Odd name, but the driver insisted you knew they would be here."

LuAnn took a deep breath and let it out slowly as she climbed into her car and turned the ignition. Suddenly the pieces came together, each one fitting but not where she expected. "Tess, is Brad there?"

"He is. Why?"

"Go get him and put him on speaker. Janice too, if you can."

"Sure," she said. After a minute she returned to the line. "Okay, we're all in the office. What's up?"

"I did not order a food truck. I don't know who's in it, but I do know the lady we need to be worried about is not the one we think it is. Call Agent Butler. I'm on my way."

"Wait. What?"

"No time. I'll explain when I get there."

LuAnn hung up the phone and dropped it into her purse, then started the car. She pressed her palm to the gearshift, then heard a noise.

"No fast moves," a deep voice said. "I got a gun. Just drive, and I'll tell you where you're going."

LuAnn looked into the rearview mirror and saw a familiar face. "Hello, Eugene."

"So you know," he said. "Did that Fed tell you?"

"No," she told him. "I figured it out by myself."

"Well, aren't you smart? Now drive. Go to the inn. I've got business there."

She did as he said, but she had her own plan once they reached the inn. Rather than turn into the front drive, she circled around.

"Hey, lady," he yelled. "I said up front."

"And I'm the one driving," she told him. "So you're riding with me."

"Amelia said you were a pain," he said. "But the other one, she actually liked you, though I can't say I see why."

"Maybe I'm just so much fun to be around."

LuAnn gunned the engine as she drove to the back of the inn. There she spied the food truck backed into the loading dock. She aimed her car for it. At the last minute, she swerved and missed the truck but stopped inches away from the truck's door to keep it from opening. The sudden move caused Eugene to tumble forward.

Meanwhile, LuAnn used the distraction to scamper out of the car. In the time it would take Eugene to figure out the child locks were enabled and he had to climb over the front seat to get out, she could alert the others.

"Eugene is outside," she said. "Brad, you're going to need to find Officer Goggan. I think I see him over at the punch bowl. Tell him to cover the back of the building. And Tess, call Agent Butler. Tell him we've got his man. And I'm pretty sure his woman too."

"What do you want me to do?" Janice asked.

"Come with me," LuAnn said. "We're going to make sure no one leaves until the Feds get here."

"Goodness gracious goat," Janice said. "I've never had this much excitement at a wedding."

LuAnn smiled as she nodded toward the back entrance. "Well, it's about to get more exciting."

"Ellie?" Janice said.

The wedding planner made an entrance that rivaled the last time she arrived at the inn. Today she wore her hair down in long beach waves, and her makeup was impeccable. In her hand was a wrapped gift.

"Just a little something for the happy couple," she said as she placed the gift on the table and turned to smile at LuAnn.

LuAnn looked past her to where her favorite FBI agent was making a much more discreet entrance. He moved across the room to join them.

"Where are we going?" Agent Butler asked.

"Back entrance," LuAnn said. "That's where the food truck is."

Agent Butler looked down at Ellie and rolled his eyes. "Must you always dress like that?"

"Only when the job calls for it," Ellie said. She removed the government-issue handgun from her jeweled handbag and nodded toward the rear entrance, then kicked off her four-inch heels. "And right now the job calls for chasing bad guys."

By the time Brad came back in, the two government agents were gone. "Was that Ellie I just saw?"

"It was," LuAnn said.

"So you found her?" Brad smiled. "Good job."

"No," LuAnn said. "She found us." She nodded to Tess and Janice. "With their help, that is."

"I'm confused," Janice said. "What did we do?"

"You solved a missing person case and brought a criminal to justice," LuAnn said. "Thanks to some facial recognition software, some persistence, and a food truck."

A few minutes later, Agent Butler returned and motioned for the women to follow him. "We've got our guy in custody. And we got our witness back. Whether she testifies or not, we've got Eugene on a whole list of charges, not the least of which is attempted kidnapping of LuAnn Sherrill."

"I will be glad to testify," she said.

Later, as the ladies tucked the last of the reception décor into boxes to be removed tomorrow, Tess asked, "How did you figure out that Ellie was not the WITSEC witness?"

LuAnn grinned. "I was thinking about what Agent Butler said about how witnesses often want to go back to their old lives because the sacrifice is too much. I tried to think of what Ellie would have missed in WITSEC, and I couldn't come up with a thing. Then I thought about Marsha. Ellie said she was from the country, and she looked miserable every time we saw her. Plus, she was the first to leave. Why would the protected witness stay and the marshal leave?"

"She wouldn't."

"Exactly," LuAnn said. "Nor would she make sure to return what she knew was important to me."

"About that," Janice said. "How did she get them into your notebook?"

"Remember when Agent Butler said he expected Ellie to be at the scene of the house explosion?" She shrugged. "She was, only her intention was to retrieve my things."

"All right," Tess said. "But the explosion. That was Gino, wasn't it?"

"It was. He had persuaded Marsha—I mean Amelia—to change her mind about testifying against him. But before they left they wanted to either kill Ellie or scare her away. So Gino used his skills and rigged up her house to explode. Amelia had stolen Ellie's cell phone before she left and called Justin. They didn't have anything against him; they just needed someone to trip the wire. Then they found out Brad was going to get his sign out of the garage. I'm sure that was the icing on the cake for them."

Janice let out a long breath and nodded. "So did Ellie really take the pictures and Grant's negatives? And your camera?"

"She did," said LuAnn. "I think as a general rule, FBI agents aren't too keen to have their pictures taken. They especially object to pictures of them with suspects. She stored the items in her house, but she had no idea Gino was going to blow it up."

Tess snapped her fingers. "And Marsha's phone lines! I bet she was just so paranoid she couldn't stand anyone having access to her that way."

LuAnn laughed. "Well, that doesn't explain Ellie's phone, but I'm inclined to believe she really did just drop it."

"So there you go," Tess said. "Another mystery solved, and a wedding added in for good measure."

"There is one more mystery we haven't solved," LuAnn said.

"And what is that?" Tess asked.

"Is the Murphey baby a girl or a boy?" Janice offered.

"There's only one way to solve that mystery," LuAnn said. "Grab your purses, Inn Crowd. We're heading to the hospital to answer the final question of the night."

It was a beautiful baby boy.

Another mystery solved.

Dear Reader,

Thank you for taking another trip to Marietta, Ohio with me! I love spending time with Janice, LuAnn, and Tess and hope you do too.

I imagine Wayfarers Inn to be a most interesting place to visit, don't you? Between the constant sleuthing and the wonderful friends and neighbors, no one would ever be bored. And speaking of fun and never being bored, I was thrilled to read about the fun things taking place in the real Marietta, namely the monthly First Friday event. In case you were wondering, yes, there really are a number of businesses open that host open houses for the public the first Friday of each month. While participation is voluntary, from what I understand, there are plenty of places to visit and goodies to sample. Many, like our fictional First Friday celebration at the inn, feature art and food as part of their fun. How great is that?

Another interesting aspect of this story was the true account of the meteor that fell near Marietta back in the 1800s. Being something of an astronomy buff, I was thrilled that I could work my love of that science into my historical tale. I hope you enjoyed it. I know I had a great time reading through all the first-hand accounts of the time period.

Again, thank you for coming along for another stay at Wayfarers Inn. I hope to see you next time!

Much love,
Kathleen Y'Barbo

ABOUT THE AUTHOR

Bestselling author Kathleen Y'Barbo is a multiple Carol Award and RITA nominee and author of more than ninety books with almost two million copies of her books in print in the US and abroad. A tenth-generation Texan and certified paralegal, she has been nominated for a Career Achievement Award as well a Reader's Choice Award and several Top Picks by *Romantic Times* magazine. She is a founding member of ACFW, Novelists Inc., and the Texas Bar Association Paralegal Division.

Kathleen celebrated her fifteenth year as a published author by receiving the *Romantic Times* Inspirational Romance Book of the Year Award for her historical romantic suspense/steampunk book *Sadie's Secret,* a novel in the Secret Lives of Will Tucker series. Her stories celebrate life, love, and the Lord—and whenever she can manage it, her home state of Texas. Recent releases include bestselling *The Pirate Bride, River of Life* (a Wayfarers Inn mystery), and *My Heart Belongs in Galveston, Texas.*

To find out more about Kathleen, sign up for her newsletter, connect with her through social media, or check out her website at kathleenybarbo.com.

A Closer Look At ... The New Concord Meteorite of 1860

May 1, 1860 began as an ordinary day in the city of New Concord and the surrounding counties. Residents went about their usual business not knowing that their average Tuesday morning was about to become an extraordinary afternoon. In fact, it is an afternoon that people are still talking about!

At approximately twenty minutes before one o'clock in the afternoon, residents as far as several counties away heard a distinct rumbling sound. Some claimed to hear whistling while others saw something streak across the sky from east to west.

In Marietta, the sound came from the north or slightly to the northeast and was described in the Memoirs of the National Academy of Sciences, Volume XIII: "Twenty-three distinct detonations were heard, after which the sounds became blended together and were compared to the rattling fire of an awkward squad of soldiers, and by others to the roar of a railway train." As the story goes, one Marietta merchant happened to be at home enjoying his lunch when the meteorites fell. He ran all the way back into the city because he was afraid a powder magazine in his store had exploded.

Owing to the lack of information about what might have happened, there was an understandable panic among those who saw or heard the event. With war looming, citizens were on edge. Some—like our fictional character Prudence—wondered if what they saw and heard in the north sky was the beginning of what they feared most.

No one was hurt by any of the falling fragments, but there were claims later—still being debated—as to whether the meteorite killed a horse. One report recorded in the local newspapers indicated that houses shook many miles away.

Men working in a field nearby heard a hissing sound followed by a rumble that turned into a roar and then, when the meteor struck the ground, the earth around them shook like an earthquake. The workers hurried to the sight and found a newly made hole in the earth with a massive rock buried two feet in the center of it.

The landing of the meteorite, dubbed locally as the Guernsey County Meteorite, was quite a spectacular event, despite the fact that overcast skies made viewing difficult in some areas. In all, more than thirty stones, the heaviest of which weighed 113 pounds, rained down on Muskingum County at a rate of one every ten to fifteen seconds for two minutes. The area where the meteorites fell, called the strewn field, was estimated at ten miles long and three miles wide. The stones were described as having a dark crust on the outside and being warm but not hot to the touch, as if the rock had been sitting in the summer sun all day.

As of the report written in 1901, Professor E.B. Andrews of Marietta College had gained possession of the 113-pound stone and delivered it to the geology department of the university for research purposes. This stone is sometimes referred to as the Main Mass. Many others were dispersed to other colleges and scientific institutions for study, but a large number of the fragments ended up in private hands. As of this writing, there was even a .054-gram New Concord meteorite fragment offered for sale on eBay!

Something Delicious from our Wayfarers Inn Friends

Meteorite Brownies

¼ cup cocoa

1 stick of butter

2 eggs

1 teaspoon vanilla

¼ cup flour

1 cup sugar

⅛ teaspoon salt

Melt butter in saucepan, add cocoa, then stir until smooth. Remove from heat and allow to cool. In a mixing bowl, whisk two eggs together, one at a time, then stir in vanilla and cooled butter and cocoa mixture. Combine dry ingredients in a separate bowl and add to the liquid mixture, stirring slowly until combined. Pour into greased 8 × 8 square baking dish and bake 25–30 minutes at 325 degrees. Let cool and cut. Brownies should be soft at the center and gooey in texture.

Optional: to simulate the texture of fallen meteors, sprinkle finished brownies with chopped nuts before cutting.

Read on for a sneak peek of another exciting book
in the Secrets of Wayfarers Inn series!

FORGET-ME-NOTS
by Tracey Bateman

February, 1863

*Though my religion bids me condemn the violence of this war, I
cannot help but justify the merits of Mr. Lincoln's actions thus
far. And as our lives have settled into a calm such as we have not
experienced in many years, I wonder if we have grown compla-
cent. No parcels have arrived in over a year, and I yearn to be of
service to those still held in bondage, despite the president's
decree of emancipation. My dear husband is well aware of my
double-minded heart. He tells me to be content rolling bandages
and gathering goods for the soldiers and the wounded, but
would the Lord have us do more? Oh, Lord, by Thy grace, I roll
my works into Thy almighty hands and trust Thee to establish
my thoughts and guide my steps.*

April 6, 1863

Despite the warmth of the sun shining down on the little spot behind the house, Prudence Willard knew it was likely a foolhardy exercise to plant a garden so early in April. But after such a long, hard winter, she couldn't bear the thought of remaining housebound. With effort, she had convinced her reluctant husband to turn the ground and make it ready for her to plant vegetables she could already envision adorning her dinner table in a couple of months.

"Thee does know the seeds thee is planting are never going to grow?"

Prudence tossed Jason a cheeky grin and shrugged. "It has been warm for over a week now. The Lord may bless us with warmth from here on out."

With a grin in return, he reached suddenly and swiped at her nose with a dirt smudged finger.

"Jason Willard!" She attempted to sound stern, despite the laughter in her voice. "Thee will pay for that."

He took off as fast as his limping leg would allow and Prudence deliberately moved slower than she was capable of running, though she knew she certainly wasn't fooling him.

Several years had passed since he'd injured himself helping a runaway slave, and he no longer became defensive about his handicap. Still, sparing him humiliation had been her task for so long, she did so instinctively. As instinctively as she protected their four-year-old son, Moses.

For Prudence, the loss of her precious baby girl soon after birth and the heartbreak of losing several babies not fully brought to term had been her cross to carry. Though she praised the Lord for their dear Moses, she had dreamed of being a mother to a brood. But the Lord had other plans for them. By His grace, they had saved countless, body and soul, from the ravages of slavery.

But for the past two years, with the war raging in the southern states, the need for their help getting slaves to the next station toward freedom had been few and far between and now it had been over a year since a new "package" had arrived. She hated the thought of the hardships they must be enduring in the south, smack in the middle of fighting. Prudence and Jason had discovered that, as difficult as it had been for slaves to escape before the war, the fighting and constant threat of being caught and conscripted into either army kept most of the slaves on the plantations, likely praying for victory for Mr. Lincoln's army.

Beneath the weight of her thoughts, Prudence realized she had stopped running after Jason altogether. He stood a couple of yards away, staring at her with a mix of compassion and exasperation.

"Thee is thinking about the war again." He closed the distance between them.

She nodded as he wrapped her in his arms and drew her close. He heaved a heavy sigh, and she knew what he was going to say. "Dear, thy heavenly Father loves His children in bondage even more than we do. They will soon be free."

Enjoying the comfort of his warm body and solid chest, she remained silent, unwilling to ruin the moment for either of them. She longed to explain the disquiet inside of her in a way that would make him understand how utterly useless she'd felt since their calling had apparently come to an end. But a high-pitched scream coming from somewhere at the front of the house made them both jump and take off running. This time, Prudence sprinted ahead of her husband, heedless of his pride as her baby boy cried for his mama.

Prudence reached Moses in only a few seconds, then stopped short at the sight that greeted her. Her heart reached her throat as she froze, staring at a snarling, half-starved bloodhound with its teeth bared at her little boy.

Tess Wallace enjoyed the aroma of her first mug of coffee for the day—fully caffeinated of course. After all, it was barely 7:15 a.m. as she left the kitchen, which was filled with the scents of bread dough, bacon, and other tantalizing breakfast foods that Winnie had begun.

She headed toward the office, but went past the room as she heard the front door open, then close. Curious, she walked to the foyer to find LuAnn unhooking Huck's leash. The former stray ran straight to Tess. She held up her hand and obediently, he sat, looking up at her expectantly, tail wagging a hundred miles a minute. With an indulgent smile, Tess bent and scratched the little dog behind his ears.

"He's wet." She glanced at LuAnn as she straightened.

"It's starting to sleet." She shivered. "*Brr*. He didn't take long out there."

Tess returned her smile. "He's up early today."

Smothering a yawn with the back of her hand, LuAnn nodded. "He heard you leave your room, I think."

"Sorry."

With a little wave, LuAnn looked toward the kitchen. "Winnie's coffee will wake me right up. Do you mind keeping an eye on Huck?"

Tess glanced at the dog, still sitting at her feet, still wagging his tail. "I don't mind, if he doesn't. I'm just going into the office to do my devotions and some paperwork."

"Thanks," LuAnn said. "I'd hate for him to run up and down the stairs this early and risk waking any of the guests. I won't be too long unless Winnie needs help."

"Good luck with that," she called after LuAnn as her friend headed toward the kitchen. "She didn't want my help." The Inn had been at nearly full capacity over the weekend and most of the guests would leave today. That meant they would want a final, full breakfast from Winnie's masterful hand before checking out. The dining room would soon be hopping.

With a glance at Huck, she turned and started to walk back toward the office. The dog would follow without a command, so she didn't offer one.

Tess wrapped her cold fingers around the mug and allowed it to begin warming her like the first rays of sun on a spring day—not that they'd had much of that over the past week. She heard the distinct sound of pinging against the windows in the foyer and, on a whim, made another detour from her intended destination. She walked toward the front door, Huck trailing, his puppy nails keeping a steady rhythm across the hardwood floor. Goodness, someone needed to take the dog to the groomer and get those claws trimmed before he scratched the finish on their beautiful floors. He sat at her feet while she pulled back the curtain covering one of the long windows to see sleet bouncing off the concrete as it hit the ground. It was ridiculous for ice to return the second week of April, but temperatures were expected to be above freezing later, so thankfully, this wouldn't last.

With a sigh, she dropped the curtain and then resumed her trek to the office. Paperwork always accumulated over the weekend, and she might as well get it caught up before the guests emerged from their rooms for breakfast.

Huck quickened his noisy little steps as he tagged along. Tess had to admit—even if only to herself—that she was glad he had joined her this dismal morning while she waited for the day to truly begin.

Just as she and Huck stepped into the office, the front bell dinged. Frowning, she halted her steps and they returned to the foyer. It was unusual for them to have guests this early, especially on such a foul-weathered morning.

An attractive, sixty-something-year-old African American man stood just inside the door, leaning heavily on a wooden cane. He looked a little unsure of himself and his posture suggested he may be contemplating leaving. As his gaze fell on Tess, relief softened his worried expression, and beneath a groomed, nearly-white mustache, his lips turned into a smile that reached his eyes. "Hello," he said. "Have I come at a bad time?"

Tess gave a dismissive wave of her hand and shook her head. "No, you're perfectly fine. We officially open the doors at eight." With a little yelp, Huck bounded around her and jumped up on the man. "I'm so sorry. Huck," she scolded. "Sit!"

The pup obeyed, but stayed firmly planted at the man's feet.

"Friendly little guy, isn't he?"

"He usually doesn't act that way. Never, actually. What can I do for you?"

She couldn't recall there being a reservation for today. She'd double-checked the computer just before bed last night. Besides, check-in wasn't until afternoon.

The man hesitated just for a beat, then reached inside his coat pocket and pulled out a folded sheet of paper. "This may seem a little odd, but I think I had a reservation here in December."

"You *think* you had a reservation?" Tess walked forward and reached for the paper.

"Well, I'm not sure, but as you can see, it appears that way."

Tess looked over pen scratches scrawling across the unlined paper. It had the name of the inn, a significant dollar amount that appeared to be equal to three month's lodging, and the date—December 1. She looked up and met his questioning gaze. How could someone not know if he'd made a reservation four months ago, paid an exorbitant amount of money, then never shown up?

She smelled a scam and narrowed her eyes, yet something familiar about the information on the page started to seep into her memory, making her second guess her knee-jerk suspicion.

"I should explain." The man gave a nod toward the paper in her hand. "In early December, I was in an accident. At least, that's what I've been told. I woke with no memories prior to the accident. And unfortunately, it's all still a blank."

Before Tess could form words or even a thought about what she'd just been told, movement from the corner of her eye caught her attention and caused her to turn. Janice Eastman held on to the wooden railing as she descended the long open steps, a pleasant smile curving her lips. "Oh, we have a guest. Good morning." She reached out a hand to the visitor and widened her smile. "I'm Janice."

"Titus Jones." He accepted her proffered hand. "Nice to meet you. As I was just telling…" He frowned a little, glancing at Tess.

"Tess," she said. "Janice and I are business partners."

"And friends for forty years," Janice said in her cheery-even-before-coffee voice. Her matching personality had won the hearts of practically everyone who had ever met the platinum blonde-haired, widowed minister's wife.

Tess handed Janice the paper. "Titus thinks he may have had a reservation in December. Why does that seem so familiar?"

Janice sucked in her bottom lip as she read, then suddenly glanced up at the man, eyes wide. She cast a glance at Tess, then back to the man.

"Tess, you remember." She looked at Titus. "You must be 'money-order man'!"

The man's eyebrows rose, but humor glinted in his eyes.

"Money-order man?" he asked. "I'm not sure..."

"He doesn't remember making the reservation or paying for it," Tess said. "Apparently, he was in an accident on the way here that day."

"Well, that would explain a lot." Janice gave the man a reassuring smile. "You've been a mystery for months."

"I apologize..."

"Oh, don't apologize. If anyone loves a mystery, it's us. Right, Tess? Besides, you couldn't help it." She shook her head. "Amnesia...it's almost like a movie!"

"It does seem like a fiction plot." He frowned. "I suppose I would describe it more as a horror flick," he said, his tone wistful.

"How insensitive of me." Reaching out, Janice touched his arm. "Tess, how can we figure out if Titus is the one who made those reservations?"

"I can look it up," Tess said. "What was the name on the reservation?"

"Titus Jones."

"You remember your name, but nothing else?"

"My identification was in my wallet," he said matter-of-factly.

"Oh, of course."

Janice shot Tess a frown that told her she was being less than gracious. And she probably was, which made her feel a twinge of doubt, especially after the sermon yesterday about being careful of how you treat strangers. She highly doubted Titus Jones was an angel sent by God, but the least she could do was check him out just in case. "I'll see what I can find," she said, using a little more accommodating tone.

Janice nodded and lifted her gaze to the tall stranger. "The café hasn't officially opened yet, but it just so happens, we know the owners. We can get you a cup of coffee. Or do you prefer tea? Or do you even remember which you prefer?"

He chuckled. "To be honest, I don't know how I felt about coffee before December, but I can say that I am more than a little fond of a good, strong cup or two in the morning. And I prefer tea in the evening."

"Good! Come on. We can probably find something for breakfast too. On the house."

"Oh, no. I couldn't..."

Tess shook her head. Janice loved to "on the house" things. Of course, she and LuAnn had given away their share of coffee, pastries, and soup too.

Predictably, Janice didn't hear a word of his protest. "A good breakfast and a cup of coffee is a must on a morning like this. Can you believe it's still all wintry out there?"

Annoyance filled Tess as Huck followed after them. The little traitor. She remained where she was, watching them walk toward the café as their voices trailed. Janice stopped and looked back. "Coming, Tess?"

She nodded. "In just a minute. I need to stop by the office and check on that reservation."

They disappeared into the café, and Tess walked the few steps to the office. She had barely turned the key in the lock, settled into the chair, and set her coffee cup on the desk when Janice appeared at the door. Tess raised her eyebrows. "What did you do with Mr. Jones?"

"Winnie is fussing over him. He gave me this." She handed over a business card. "He thought it might help you confirm his story."

Tess glanced at the card.

"It's his psychiatrist," Janice said. "She's been working with him to recover memories since the medical doctors can't find a physical reason for his amnesia. I feel pretty sure he's our mystery man from December. And I have to say, you seem awfully suspicious. I think you're making him uncomfortable. Which isn't very nice."

"I'm just checking his reservation. If he's the same man, we'll give him back his money order, and he can be on his way."

"At least give the man the benefit of checking out his story before you suspect him of lying."

"I know. But you have to admit we've dealt with a lot of shady characters these past few months."

The frown lines between Janice's eyes softened. "Well, I suppose you have a point. Still... Huck is really taken with him, and you know they say if a dog likes someone, then he must a good person. Dogs can sense that kind of thing."

Affection for her soft-hearted friend surged in Tess's chest. She refrained from snarking back that a dog would follow anyone who gave him a smile and a scratch. "I'll look up the amount of the money order and confirm the date he was supposed to check in."

"What about the doctor?"

Tess set the card on her desk next to her coffee cup, which seemed to be the safest place to set anything she didn't want to lose.

"It's a little early in the day to call a professional, don't you think?"

Janice grinned. "You'd have to *need* a professional to call one this early."

Tess returned the grin. "You'd better go check on our guest before Winnie forces him to eat a little of everything she's been cooking. You know food is her love language."

"I'm going." Janice hesitated. "You're coming though, right? LuAnn should be down soon."

"Ten minutes. Tops. I promise. Besides, Lu's already up."

Janice's eyebrows rose. "She is?"

"Huck was an early riser."

Janice chuckled as she walked away.

When she was once again alone in her office, Tess opened her file-folder drawer and found the envelope marked

INVALID ADDRESS. When it had become apparent their guest would not be arriving, she had attempted to return the money order to the address she'd been given, only to have it come back a week later.

Tess, herself, had taken the reservation, and though she normally wouldn't have made it without a credit card, she had been moved with compassion when she discovered the guest was a widower needing a little time away to process his grief. She certainly had understood that. The reservation had come in just around the anniversary of Jeffrey's death. She found the four-month-old file and confirmed that the information on the paper matched the computer and the amount of the money order.

Her eye caught the card containing the number for Titus Jones's psychiatrist. She shrugged. There was really no point in calling since the rest of the information checked out. But as she shut off the light and locked the office door, she couldn't shake the questions niggling her brain. The information had technically checked out, but had it really? Amnesia might explain their visitor's whereabouts for the past four months, but it didn't explain why he had given them an invalid address in the first place.

A NOTE FROM THE EDITORS

We hope you enjoy Secrets of Wayfarers Inn, created by the Books and Inspirational Media Division of Guideposts, a nonprofit organization that touches millions of lives every day through products and services that inspire, encourage, help you grow in your faith, and celebrate God's love in every aspect of your daily life.

Thank you for making a difference with your purchase of this book, which helps fund our many outreach programs to military personnel, prisons, hospitals, nursing homes, and educational institutions. To learn more, visit Guideposts Foundation.org.

We also maintain many useful and uplifting online resources. Visit Guideposts.org to read true stories of hope and inspiration, access OurPrayer network, sign up for free news-letters, download free e-books, join our Facebook community, and follow our stimulating blogs.

To learn about other Guideposts publications, including the best-selling devotional *Daily Guideposts*, go to ShopGuideposts .org, call (800) 932-2145, or write to Guideposts, PO Box 5815, Harlan, Iowa 51593.

Sign up for the
Guideposts Fiction Newsletter
and stay up-to-date on
the books you love!

You'll get sneak peeks of new releases, recommendations from other Guideposts readers, and special offers just for you . . .
and it's FREE!

Just go to Guideposts.org/Newsletters today to sign up.

Find more inspiring fiction in these best-loved Guideposts series!

Tearoom Mysteries Series

Mix one stately Victorian home, a charming lakeside town in Maine, and two adventurous cousins with a passion for tea and hospitality. Add a large scoop of intriguing mystery and sprinkle generously with faith, family, and friends, and you have the recipe for *Tearoom Mysteries.*

Sugarcreek Amish Mysteries

Be intrigued by the suspense and joyful "aha" moments in these delightful stories. Each book in the series brings together two women of vastly different backgrounds and traditions, who realize there's much more to the "simple life" than meets the eye.

Mysteries of Martha's Vineyard

What does Priscilla Latham Grant, a Kansas farm girl know about hidden treasure and rising tides, maritime history and local isle lore? Not much—but to save her lighthouse and family reputation, she better learn quickly!

Mysteries of Silver Peak

Escape to the historic mining town of Silver Peak, Colorado, and discover how one woman's love of antiques helps her solve mysteries buried deep in the town's checkered past.

**To learn more about these books,
visit Guideposts.org/Shop**